MW01233663

DOUBLE STANDARD

FOR DANIELLE, I HOPE
YOU LIKE THE BOOK!

Ruth Woodling

RUTH WOODLING

This is a work of fiction and any resemblance to
persons living or dead is purely coincidental.

Print ISBN: 978-1-66786-305-4
eBook ISBN: 978-1-66786-306-1

Many thanks to Rosalind Route, Karen Heroy, Caitlin Jones, Catherine Woodling, Ruth Cook and Walter Kruger for their help and encouragement. They all played a part in making the book better.

CHAPTER ONE

Marilyn glanced around the courtroom. It was packed. She approached the bailiff and asked him how many media passes had been issued. He said all of them. John Drummond, one of the local TV anchors she knew from other high-profile cases, caught her eye and smiled. She smiled back.

She leaned over to Rene. "You're going to be on the evening news."

Marilyn Harris had been Rene's attorney since she met her at a cocktail party several years ago. Marilyn had resolved Rene's legal issues then, but knew she would be hearing from Rene again. Rene was just too good looking and talented not to get her rear in a wringer down the road in the male-dominated surgery world.

Marilyn knew that even though Judge Weldon had banned cameras from the courtroom, it was likely that there would be cameras in the hall and outside the courthouse. She thought this was especially true because of Drummond's presence.

Rene looked surprised. "How do they even know what the case is about?" she asked.

"They send interns out to scour the dockets to find the interesting cases. This is obviously not your run-of-the-mill contract case."

Marilyn had warned Rene about the possible publicity, but Rene had not really taken it in until now.

"Will they be here every day?"

"You can count on it."

"Will they want to talk to me?"

"For sure, but I'm here to run interference for you. No talking to the media until after the verdict. But you're going to smile that beautiful smile at all of them." She knew that smile had saved Rene in the past. She just had to be reminded to flash it.

The parties had summarized their arguments for the jury in their opening statements. The attorneys and the parties were seated at the counsel tables in the front of the courtroom. It was time to hear from the witnesses.

Marilyn looked at Rene. "Take a deep breath and fasten your seatbelt. Here we go." Marilyn had told Rene that she would be asking her questions she might find embarrassing, because if she didn't get there first, the defendants would.

"Your Honor, the Plaintiff calls Dr. Rene James."

Rene made her way to the witness stand next to Judge Weldon. The clerk swore her in.

"Raise your right hand. Do you swear to tell the truth, the whole truth and nothing but the truth?"

"I do."

"Dr. James, please state your full name for the record."

"Rene Elizabeth James."

"What is your profession?"

"I'm a physician."

"When did you graduate from medical school?"

"1995."

"Where did you go to medical school?"

"Northwestern University in Chicago."

"What is your medical specialty?"

"My specialty is plastic surgery with a subspecialty in facial reconstruction."

"How did you decide on that specialty?"

"When I was in my residency, I had a little girl as a patient who was born with deformed facial features. I believed I could give her a normal face, which my team and I succeeded in doing. That's where my interest began."

"Am I correct that you have a national reputation as a facial reconstruction surgeon?"

"I'm afraid someone else will have to answer that question."

"Have the news media covered your career?"

"Yes."

"How often have you been the subject of media coverage?"

"Many times."

"More than a dozen?"

"Yes."

"In fact, *60 Minutes* did a segment on your work with veterans of the Afghan War, did it not?"

3

"Yes."

"Do you also hold a position at Kenton Medical School?

"Yes, I'm an Associate Professor in the Medical School."

"That's a tenured position, is it not?"

"Yes."

"So to summarize, you are a well-known facial reconstruction surgeon who is a tenured professor at Kenton Medical School, would that be correct?"

"Yes."

"So how do men react to you in social situations?"

"They find me intimidating."

"Why do you think that is?"

"Again, I'm afraid you will have to ask someone else that question."

"Is it possible that it's because you are a nationally known surgeon and a tenured university professor?"

"Yes, it's possible."

"Do you have any friends who have had similar experiences?"

"Yes, I have one woman friend who is a Harvard Business School graduate. She says that when she tells men in social situations about her education, they literally turn and walk away. She calls it 'The H Bomb.' I also have another woman friend who is a lawyer. She say she tells the men she meets she is a paralegal. Otherwise, they never ask her out."

"So regardless of the reason for what you have identified as your being intimidating, have you taken any action to deal with it?"

"Yes."

"What action would that be?"

"A couple years ago when I turned 50, I decided that I wasn't going to spend the rest of my life without male companionship. At the beginning of each semester, the administration invited me to welcome the residents to the medical school. That year, I identified three of the residents whom I wanted to get to know better and gave them a small piece of paper with my name and telephone number on it along with the word 'Dinner.'"

"Did any of them call you?"

"As a matter of fact, they all did."

"So what did you tell them?"

"I invited each of them to my house for dinner."

"Individually?"

"Yes, and they all showed up."

"So what happened then?"

"We had dinner and then went to bed."

"When you say you 'went to bed,' what do you mean?"

"We had sex."

"Did you initiate the sex?"

"It was mutual."

"And you had sex with all of them?"

"Yes."

"Did you see any of them again?"

"All of them. We would get together every week or so during the semester depending on our schedules."

"What happened at the end of the semester?"

"Our meetings ended. I had made it clear and they had agreed that whatever relationship we had wasn't meant to be permanent. I was at least 20 years older than they were."

"Let me ask you, didn't you see an issue with the power imbalance between you as a tenured professor and these residents?"

"No, because I made it crystal clear to every one of them from the beginning that it was all totally voluntary. And I never gave an invitation to anyone whom I directly supervised. Plus, when I told my then chief I was pregnant and that the father was a resident, he told me he knew I'd had relationships with residents. When I asked him why he hadn't spoken to me about it, he smiled and said he had never, ever gotten a complaint." The jury laughed.

"So with the new semester, the process began again?"

"Yes."

"And for how many semesters did this go on?"

"Five."

"Why did it stop?"

"For whatever reason, my birth control stopped working properly and I got pregnant. I think it's because I'm going through menopause."

"And you're pregnant now?"

"Yes."

"So you decided to keep the baby?"

"Yes. Obviously." The jury chuckled.

"When is the baby due?"

"In about a month. It's a girl." She smiled.

CHAPTER TWO

"Are we ready?" Rene asked her surgical team.

It was 7:00 a.m. and Rene was already scrubbed in for surgery. As her mother had often said, "If you're on time, you're late." It was a mantra she had long ago adopted as her own. Over her more than 20 years as a surgeon, Rene had developed a habit of arriving at least fifteen minutes before she was required to report to the operating room. She used the time to clear her head and visualize the hours ahead.

She had first become interested in becoming a doctor in a biology course in high school. Ms. Miller's 9th grade class had sparked her interest in medicine. She was fascinated by the intricacy and beauty of the human body. She never took lightly the fact that she could play a role in shaping it.

There were many educated women in her family, so there was no pushback, only encouragement. She was now nationally recognized by many as the best in her field.

Rachel Snyder was a seven year old girl whose face had been disfigured when a drunk driver ran through a red light and plowed into the side of her parents' car. Her family had done their research and had learned that Rene was the best facial reconstruction surgeon anywhere. Rene often thought of her first patient while operating. She had grown up and married and now had children, which Rene felt she had helped make possible.

She had the perfect hands for a surgeon. Delicate with long, slender fingers, although it didn't matter as much anymore because of all the electronic and robotic equipment that had been developed over the last several years and which she used with such skill.

She was also known for the warmth of the relationships she developed with her patients, something unusual for surgeons. She had met with this little girl more than once in the hospital to introduce herself, to explain what she was planning to accomplish, and to review what was going to happen in the operating room and during recovery. She was known for asking her colleagues "What is the very best we can do for this patient?"

She had asked for Dr. Banfield, an anesthesiologist she knew to be not only very skilled, but also conversational with her patients. The little girl would be frightened, and Rene wanted the anesthesiologist, who would be the first doctor she would interact with on the morning of the surgery, to calm her as much as possible.

Rene also had an aesthetic sense that was critical for a reconstructive surgeon. She had to be able to visualize what the final result would be and how to achieve it. Sometimes, depending on the extent of the injury, that would involve taking cartilage and skin from other parts of the patient's body. That was the case here. The cartilage was specifically necessary for reconstruction of the child's nose. Rene tried to avoid the use of artificial prostheses and was very skilled at using the patient's actual tissues to accomplish the rebuilding. She believed it made for a more natural looking result, which was particularly important with the face.

She took a deep breath.

"Scalpel."

The operation took ten hours. Her lunch was a smoothie a nurse held for her to drink through a straw. Her experience told her that the operation was successful, although the swelling would make it hard for those not familiar with similar operations to tell until a few days later.

She took off her surgical gown and equipment, walked down the hall and stepped into the waiting room to speak to the parents.

"Everything went very well. There will be some substantial swelling for the next couple days, but from my experience, it looks very good." Rene reached over and hugged the mother, who had begun to cry. "We'll keep you informed on her progress. I think you'll be pleased."

One of the residents who had been in the operating room to observe walked over to her.

"Congratulations, Dr. James. Amazing job."

"Thanks. I hope we've given her a normal life."

"Would you like to get something to eat?"

He wasn't shy, she thought.

"Yes, I'm starving, but I've ordered in at the house. Would you like to join me? What's your name?"

"Teddy Ryan. And I'd like that."

She looked at him carefully. He had almost perfect features and it was her job to remember them. He also had unusual green eyes. She wondered whether anyone else in his family had them.

Rene had ordered a 7:30 delivery from El Bandito, the best Mexican place in town. Her housekeeper, Faye, had taken Jake, her black lab, home with her because she knew Rene would be late and tired. Rene had never considered a dog because of her schedule, but then she had received a call from the parents of one of her former patients. He was in the military and had been killed while deployed to Afghanistan. Much to her surprise, his parents told her that he had wanted her to have his dog if anything happened to him. She couldn't say no. Jake was smart and friendly, and he and Faye also hit it off, so it was a done deal.

Rene was a regular at the restaurant, and they knew she liked her food hot and fresh, so they were right on time. There was plenty for both of them.

"This is as close to the real thing as you can find," said Rene.

"So you've been to Mexico."

"Yes, many times."

"Do you speak Spanish?"

"Enough to get by. How about you?"

"Some. I've never been to Mexico, but I was an exchange student in a university town outside Madrid called Alcala de Henares. It's the birthplace of Cervantes."

Interesting guy, she thought. He actually knows who Cervantes is.

"So how did you decide to become a doctor?"

"Good question. My father wanted me to go into the family business, which has been very successful, and he has been more than a little disappointed with my choice. But he had a heart attack several years ago, which brought about my interest in medicine."

"Yes, your specialty is cardio-thoracic surgery, is it not?"

"Yes, and that's the connection. So, how about you? You're well known for your specialty. How did that come about?"

She and Teddy talked about her career and how it had developed, which he found fascinating and encouraging.

"Listen, I really appreciate your hospitality and the food was delicious," said Teddy, "but I know you're exhausted, so I'm going to be on my way."

"Before you go, and I know this is an odd request, but I need a hot bath, and I wondered whether you'd draw one for me."

He hesitated. She looked at him and flashed a smile.

"Of course. I'd be happy to."

"There's a tub in the master bath down the hall, and some lavender bath oil on the counter."

He walked down the hall and started the bath. He went back to the kitchen to get her.

"There are fresh towels and hair ties in the cupboard. My robe is on the hook behind the door, if you'd get it down for me."

They walked together down the hall. He held her robe up high and she got undressed behind it and got in the tub. He handed her the hair ties, trying not to embarrass her by looking at her. The tub was large and freestanding and the water covered all of her up to her shoulders.

"Give me about 20 twenty minutes."

"Sure. I'll check on you then."

He checked on her in 20.

"I'm ready." He held her robe up again and she slipped into it. Her face was flushed, which made her look even more attractive.

"You wouldn't know, but it's very hard to be alone after a day like this. Would you mind staying?"

It was clear to him that he was being seduced, and he was enjoying it. He knew he wasn't the first. He stepped over to her and kissed her. Her lips were warm and soft and she smelled like lavender. He opened the door to the bedroom. She kissed him again. He turned down the covers on the large, high bed, lifted her in, and got in next to her. She helped him take off his clothes and pressed herself against him. He slid into her easily as she gave him another deep kiss.

They both knew that first time sex wasn't always the best, but they sensed that this was different. They were a perfect fit for each other. No discomfort, only pleasure, something she needed right then more than he knew. He moved slowly at first to make it last longer, but finally lost control and took her with him. She called out his name when they came, which was very unusual for her.

"Jesus, Rene, that was spectacular," he said, still out of breath.

"Yes, it was," she admitted. She wondered whether the young girls he was screwing knew anything about sex.

The sun was coming up. She sat up, slipped on his shirt and walked into the kitchen. She thought she would be tired, but, surprisingly, she wasn't. The kitchen was large and beautiful, with marble countertops and gleaming appliances, but not often used except for her quick breakfasts and takeout orders. She had bought the house as an investment, but seldom used anything but the kitchen, her bedroom, and the family room, which she had hired a decorator to deal with. There was a pool in the back that she paid to maintain, but never swam in. Her black Mercedes sedan sat alone in the three-car garage.

She grabbed a hardboiled egg out of the fridge and popped two pieces of bread into the toaster.

He followed her into the kitchen, brushed her hair back and kissed her on the neck.

"Marry me," he whispered.

Not again, she thought.

"I'm flattered".

"I'm serious."

"I know you are. Hardboiled egg or are you a cereal guy?" she asked, taking a bite out of her toast.

"Neither."

"Oh, shit, Teddy, are you working this morning? You're already late!" She didn't like late.

"No, I'm not late".

"From here?" She tossed him his shirt. God, she was beautiful, "Shoes and pants are in the bedroom. I'll call the Uber."

He was dressed and out the door in five. No kiss. No time.

She walked into the bathroom and checked herself out in the mirror. She had a half an hour he didn't have. She was in her early 50's, but looked 30. She was slender with slim hips and Goldilocks breasts: Not too big, not too small, just right. Her eyes were a deep blue-gray that betrayed her German grandfather. Her long hair was auburn. She had never married or had children, which she was sure helped. Sometimes she had second thoughts, but it was too late now, although she still had to be careful. No getting pregnant by her young residents.

No makeup necessary and she couldn't wear it anyway. She took a quick shower and pulled the usual blouse and pants out of the closet. Nothing fancy under the scrubs.

She pulled into her parking spot with fifteen minutes to spare and took the elevator up to the fourth floor operating theater. She changed into her scrubs and double capped her long hair. She walked to the operating room and there he was, in his scrubs and ready to go.

"Good morning, Dr. Ryan, how are you this morning?" She could still feel him between her legs.

"Great, Dr. James, how about you?"

"Never better. We have a complicated jaw reconstruction this morning. You ready?"

"Always ready to learn from the best."

She knew he was bullshitting her, but she liked it. He stood next to her in the scrub area and brushed up against her ass.

"Don't ever do that again," she said under her breath.

"Got it," he said and stepped farther away.

The operating room, which was large and ice cold, was full of other assisting residents and faculty who wanted to watch her work. The operation lasted five hours. Nothing more difficult than the face, Teddy thought, but it was clear she was dazzling in her ability and knowledge. Lucky patient. Lucky residents.

"So what did you learn?"

"That you have beautiful hands."

"You need to pay more attention," she said smiling. "Thursday?"

"Whenever you want."

"That's when I want. See you then."

CHAPTER THREE

The nurses knew she would be at the reception the first week the returning residents came in. She always came by to greet the residents and welcome them back to the program. She was a superstar in the surgery world and hard not to notice because of her striking good looks. The department heads liked the fact that she made herself visible at the beginning of the year. They knew some of these residents had originally chosen the program because of her.

The nurses also knew, however, that she had other motives. She carried a small notepad with her. She was making a decision like a baseball coach on which ones to draft to fuck her during the coming months. Three or four of them would get a piece of paper from her with her name and telephone number on it, along with the word "Dinner." No one objected. Some of them were already familiar with the right of passage and disappointed when they weren't chosen. They knew, however, that they still had a shot, since complete discretion was required, and any resident who breached it in even the smallest way was immediately replaced.

The first one up to bat that semester was Sonny Mastrangelo from Chicago. His family owned several restaurants, and they had expected him to go into the family business, but one of his high school science teachers had recognized his abilities and encouraged him to go in another direction. He had graduated from college with honors and was accepted to several medical schools. He chose the University of Miami because of the warm weather.

He had all the prerequisites: tall, dark, and very good looking. She was curious, however, whether that made him a better lover or a worse one, since he wouldn't have to exert much effort to get a woman in the sack and might well be more interested in pleasing himself rather than her. She knew he had to be smart or he wouldn't be a resident.

He showed up at her door right on time with what looked like a nice bottle of red wine. Button-down shirt, khakis, and loafers. She had on a pair of black yoga pants and a white shirt. She couldn't wear anything that made her look unattractive, so she didn't have to exert much effort. She thought it was probably the same for him. He was one of those men to whom many things came easily because of their good looks.

He handed her the wine. "I hope this will work. It's a really nice Italian."

She examined it as if she knew what she was looking at and smiled. "Montepulciano. One of my favorites." She lied.

She was leaning up against the kitchen island.

"So what's for dinner?"

She looked straight at him. "I don't cook."

He looked surprised at first and then amused at his own gullibility. Everyone in his family cooked. He wasn't used to being taken, but, as an Italian, he wasn't sure that being taken by a beautiful woman was such a bad thing.

He walked over to her and kissed her. He turned her back towards the refrigerator and pushed her up against it. He pulled her pants down over her slim hips and gave her head. She took a sharp breath, put her hands in his hair and pulled him tight against her.

He knew what he was doing, so she came quickly. He reached up, popped the buttons off her shirt, ran his tongue up her belly and kissed her hard as he pushed himself inside her.

"You taste good," he whispered.

"Yes, I can tell." She could taste herself on his mouth.

He knew he had just gotten her right to the edge when he picked her up and carried her into the bedroom where they came and then did it again.

"You've done this before," she said when she finally caught her breath.

"I thought that's why you picked me, and I didn't want to disappoint you."

"Oh, you didn't."

"What kind of fast food do you like?" They both laughed.

"The world's most famous fast food is Italian. What do you like on your pizza?"

"Everything."

"Even anchovies?"

"Yes, definitely."

"My mother would love you."

"What's her name?"

"Francesca. Francesca Mastrangelo."

"Beautiful name, but hard to fit on a driver's license."

"She's a beautiful woman."

She looked him up and down. "I bet."

CHAPTER FOUR

She could tell he was a breast man the first time he looked at her. Women know the look. Just a little below her face. She did have nice breasts.

Bobby Bergman was good looking in a Midwestern sort of way. Broad face, bright blue eyes direct from Scandinavia, and a disarming smile. He had grown up on a farm in Nebraska and nobody in his family had ever been a professional. His academic abilities had become evident early on, however, and he had been encouraged to leave the farm to the other members of his family.

She hadn't had anyone focus on her breasts for a while and she was ready. "So tomorrow at 8:00?" Dinner was always late for her, even though she knew dinner wasn't exactly what was going to happen. "Bring something you'd like to drink." She was sure it would be beer, which she didn't drink.

He showed up a little after 8:00 in a long-sleeved shirt and a tie. She knew she was old enough to be his mother, but she found the attempt at some sort of formality amusing.

"Brought some Heineken. Goes with almost everything."

"Great. There should be room in the fridge."

He turned as he closed the door to the fridge and she kissed him. She was a really good kisser. He put his arms around her and returned the kiss hard and deep as if he'd been expecting it. She leaned in and kissed him back.

He unbuttoned her blouse just as she expected as they walked to the bedroom still kissing. She had worn her front clasp bra on purpose. He undid it on the bed, took her left breast in his mouth and ran his tongue around her hard nipple. He sucked on it until he could tell she was close to coming.

"Not yet. The other one first." He obliged until she said, "Now." He massaged her left nipple with his fingers and sucked hard on her right as she came.

"Oh, Jesus, where did you learn that?"

"Not on the farm."

"Are you sure it wasn't a dairy farm?" she said laughing.

"We had machines for that."

"I'm sure the cows are disappointed. Your turn. What would you like?"

"Take down your hair."

She rolled over on top of him and pulled the tie out of her long hair. It dropped down over her shoulders and his as she kissed him and he slid inside her.

He was a large man, six feet two and muscular, but he was surprisingly gentle with her, which provided a long ramp up to their orgasm that she hadn't anticipated. He had no body hair above his waist, which she found oddly erotic. A vestige of the Vikings, perhaps?

"You're not what I expected," she whispered.

"You're everything I expected."

CHAPTER FIVE

She was sitting on the exam table.

"I don't know what it is, Gerry. I'm just tired all the time, especially in the morning. Am I anemic? Is there a bug going around?"

Gerry Weinstein was Rene's age and was recommended to her years ago as the best internist around. If anyone would know, she thought, Gerry would. If he weren't so short, she would have been interested, although his family would have objected since she wasn't Jewish.

"How long have I been your personal physician, Rene?"

"Forever."

"And you almost always tell me when something is going on with you, right?"

"Right."

"So what's going on now?"

"Nothing."

"Oh, I think there is, because you're pregnant."

"What are you talking about? That's impossible. I'm scrupulous, scrupulous about birth control!"

"We've talked about the fact that you're going through menopause. You're a physician. You know what that means. Your entire system is doing unpredictable things. So, who is the father?"

Silence.

"Rene, you're not telling me you don't know."

"I've slept with several different men in the last couple months."

"You're kidding."

"Nope."

"So, who are these potential fathers?"

"Residents."

"In their 30s?"

"Yes."

"You're kidding."

"Still not kidding."

"You've got to know you've got some serious questions to answer over the next week."

"Gerry, you've got to know my head is still spinning."

"I understand."

"Do you, really? I'm 52 years old and not married."

"Look, Rene, you're in great shape. I don't see any reason you wouldn't be able to carry this pregnancy to term. And there are lots of tests now to make sure. So that inquiry is off the table. The next question is whether you want a child, because if you do, this is, in all probability, your last shot. And then, of course, there is the impact this would have on what can only be described as an incredible career. I don't envy you."

"Would you deliver the baby?"

"You know I would, although I might need some help."

"Can you identify the father from the amniotic fluid?"

"Yes."

"So, what do you need?"

"Blood, half-eaten cheeseburger, semen."

She laughed. "That I can obviously get. For what it's worth, they've all proposed."

"Pardon me, Rene, but you must be one good fuck."

She smiled, "Must be."

"When can we tell whether it's a boy or a girl?"

"Do you care?"

"Just want to know."

"Eleven weeks. You're probably around eight."

"I guess most men would still want a boy."

"Not sure. You'd make a beautiful girl."

"When do I need to get back to you on what I want to do?"

"Yesterday."

"For real."

"Clearly as soon as possible."

"You'll take care of everything?"

"Of course."

CHAPTER SIX

She had no close female friends and she couldn't tell her mother, who was still paranoid about her getting pregnant when she wasn't married, so she was on her own with this decision. She had to decide very soon if she was going to terminate the pregnancy. First, she wanted to find out who the lucky father was, although she wasn't sure it really mattered. And when she found out, she had to decide whether to tell him. She couldn't imagine a resident being thrilled with the news. She imagined Sonny was Catholic, so that would be another issue.

She took a walk. She only needed some sort of DNA from two of them. She thought there might still be a beer bottle in the trash, which would be enough for Bobby. That left Sonny and Teddy. They were both on her schedule for another "visit," but not soon enough for this. She tried to remember when the trash collection was scheduled. She hadn't made them wear a condom since she was on the pill, which, in hindsight, had been a mistake for a couple of reasons. She thought about the duvet, but Faye had taken it to the cleaners.

She called Teddy. "Hi, I need some company tonight. Would you be available?"

"I have dinner with a friend, but I'll cancel." She'd never made a request like that before, but he was already in love with her at this point, so he didn't question what was going on. He just wanted her.

She couldn't help musing about what this baby would look like if she decided to keep it. Sonny was dark, Bobby was blond, and Teddy was in the middle. All three were good looking, so that wasn't an issue.

She knew she needed to stop thinking about it because it was interfering with the decision. The question was whether she could continue with delicate all-day surgeries when she was big pregnant. And whether the chief would think so. She knew they couldn't fire her because she was pregnant, but they sure could make her life more difficult. She needed to do some quick research. Luckily, research was her thing. She also had a very good lawyer.

Teddy rang the bell.

"Door's open."

No question that he was an attractive man, and she could tell from the way he dressed that he had been to the right schools. She didn't know much else about him, except that he was good in bed. Maybe that was enough.

She actually was in the kitchen attempting to cook. He wasn't sure what that meant, but he couldn't help smiling as he walked over and kissed her.

"Thought we'd eat in. Got the recipe online. It looked easy. Can you cook?"

"Actually, I'm not bad. It's just chemistry. Let me take a look."

She was right that it was a pretty simple pasta recipe. She had the water boiling, which was the correct first step. He found the ingredients for the sauce in the fridge, which Rene had asked Faye to pick up at the grocery store.

Faye Coleman wasn't your usual housekeeper. She had worked for the president of the university for years until he had retired and moved to Florida. She had often traveled with him, acting more like a personal aide than a housekeeper. Rene had wondered whether there was something more to the relationship, but figured if there were, Faye would have a better understanding of her arrangements. Rene knew Faye from her contacts with the president and snapped her up immediately. Faye was perfect for Rene. Smart, observant, and savvy. They hit it off right away.

He threw the ingredients for the sauce in the skillet and checked the pasta for doneness.

"Got any salad greens?"

"Yes, I do," she said proudly. "I even found a bowl."

"Can you cut up the cucumbers and tomatoes?" He couldn't imagine that she couldn't, and she did so with precision. He found it very entertaining that she was attempting all this for him, although he really didn't understand what was going on. She had never shown any interest in the kitchen except to fuck him on the countertop, which was fine with him.

She poured sparkling water into crystal glasses and served the pasta and salad on what he recognized as fine China, which he was sure she'd never had out of the cupboard. The pasta was surprisingly good. He offered to clean up, but she insisted on doing it herself. He had left some food on his plate, which she set aside.

She came back to the table and sat down in the chair next to him.

"Dessert?" she asked, putting her hand on his thigh.

He picked her up and carried her into the bedroom. Her body felt more tense than usual, but he knew he could take care of that. They had their usual great sex, although he sensed that she was preoccupied with something.

She wanted to make sure Gerry had everything he needed.

"What's going on?" he finally asked.

"Nothing."

"I know that's not true. Your body is telling me otherwise. You know I'm in love with you."

"You've never told me that."

"I thought it was obvious. I'm telling you now."

"I wish you wouldn't have."

CHAPTER SEVEN

"**R**eady to find out? Want to sit down?"

She was in Gerry's office.

"No, I'm okay." She was a grown ass woman, as one of her mother's friends would say.

"It's Teddy."

"You're sure?"

"Positive. You gave me the best stuff on him. Pasta and semen." They both laughed. She sat down.

"Shit, Gerry, what now?"

"He's young and healthy, so now it's up to you. Do you want to let him know or not?"

"Not sure. He says he's in love with me."

"I don't know whether that makes it easier or harder. Would you marry him?"

"No."

"Why not."

"I'm at least 20 years older than he is, and his family would have a fit."

"Do you know anything about his family?"

"No, although I understand they are well off. I'm sure he's the Golden Boy."

"Do you think he'll acknowledge the child if you decide to go through with this?"

"No clue. I think I am going to ask him what he wants to do. His career is just beginning, and he very well may not be ready for a child. In fact, I may not be ready for a child, which is another question, isn't it?"

"When will you speak with him?"

"Tonight. You know I have to decide as soon as I can."

She called Teddy as soon as she left Gerry's office. "Teddy, I know this is getting old, but I wonder if you could come over tonight. No cooking."

He laughed. "What time?"

"Any time after 7:00. Call me when you're on the way."

"I'll be there at 7:30. What can I bring? You have to eat."

"Just yourself. See you then."

He was on her doorstep at 7:30. He had known something was going on when he saw her last, but he still had no clue, and he was worried since it was so unlike her. She was unfailingly cool and predictable, which is what made her a great surgeon.

"Thanks for coming on such short notice. There's something I have to discuss with you. I've found out I'm pregnant and we've confirmed that you're the father."

"You're kidding."

"No, unfortunately not."

"You do know that's terrific, right?"

"What? Think about it first."

"Nothing to think about. I'm in love with you and you're having my baby."

"I haven't decided whether to go through with it yet."

"You can't be serious."

"Of course I am. I'm 52 years old and have a career that's more than demanding. I haven't decided. I'm only telling you as a courtesy."

"A courtesy? What do I have to do to get you to keep it? I've already asked you to marry me."

"That's not the answer, and would only create an uproar at the school."

"Do you really think I give a shit? We're talking about someone I love and my baby."

"It's my decision, not yours. I'll let you know what I decide."

CHAPTER EIGHT

"Teddy, how soon can you get here? Fifteen? Great."

She knew if she decided to end the pregnancy, he was gone, and she wanted to see him one more time. She hadn't sorted out her feelings for him yet, but knew she cared about him and the fact that he cared about her.

He stood on the steps with a look on his face she hadn't seen before.

"Don't talk," she said. "Just make love to me."

They didn't make it past the sofa. He knew where all her buttons were at this point, and he pushed them all. He knew this might be the last time, too.

"Have you decided?"

"No."

"When?"

"Tomorrow."

"I want to stay with you."

"No, you can't. This has got to be my decision."

She knew if she ended the pregnancy, she could just pick up where she had left off with everything as far as her work was concerned. The question remained, however, whether she wanted a child and how much, because now she had the reality of one in her belly. She had come to terms with being childless years ago and believed her contributions to others' lives made up for it. She wasn't sure that had changed.

But now she found herself asking more basic questions. How long would she be able to stand, and would she even be able to reach around her belly? Would she have serious issues because of her age? Her career had been spectacular and was she willing to take a chance on trashing it for a baby? And what happens afterwards? Who would be the primary caretaker for this child? Did she want a child she would have so little time for?

As soon as Teddy left, Rene called Gerry. She got his voice-mail. "Gerry, Rene. I don't want you to decide for me. I just want to hear the familiar voice of someone who knows what I'm struggling with. I don't have anyone else I can talk to about this." He picked up his phone.

"You know I'm here whatever you need me for. When are you going to decide? Tomorrow? You're a physician. You know you can't wait much longer."

"That's the plan." She knew she was looking at her last chance. Ever.

"I know you're well informed at this point, but in case you missed it, a woman's blood volume doubles during pregnancy, which makes her more resilient rather than less."

He wasn't supposed to advise her, but he just had.

"Thanks for your friendship, Gerry."

CHAPTER NINE

"Do you have a minute, Barry?"

"For you Rene, of course." Barry Ross was the Chief of Surgery who had brought her with him to Kenton. The word had always been that he was fucking her, and her immediate boss could never deal with that, even though it wasn't true.

"I need to tell you something important. I'm pregnant."

"You've got to be kidding." He knew her age and he knew for sure she wasn't stupid.

"I'm afraid not."

"How did you let that happen?"

"Menopause. I always use birth control. I'm sure Alice has gone through the same thing." Alice was his wife and around the same age, and she liked her enough never to consider sleeping with her husband, even though she knew she could have.

"So, what are you going to do about it?"

"As you might imagine, I've thought about that quite a bit, and the answer is nothing."

"Are you saying you're going to keep it?"

"Yes, I'm going to keep it." That was the first time she'd said it out loud.

"Rene, you really must think more carefully about this. Have you considered what operating when you're in your last trimester will be like?"

"No fun, that's for sure, but I've decided that I can figure it out. With some help from you and the rest of the staff, of course."

"I'm not sure what that would be."

"I'll let you know," she said with a smile.

"Who is the father? Anyone I know?"

"Yes, Teddy Ryan."

"Well, I guess your resident habit finally caught up with you."

"What's that supposed to mean?"

"It's no secret that you've had relationships with residents. You must know that."

"Well, if you knew that, why didn't you do something about it? You're the chief."

He put his hands on his desk. "Do you want to know the honest to God truth, Rene?"

"Sure."

"I never got a complaint. Never. Ever. Pardon my putting it this way, but you obviously were magic in the sack."

She was shocked and flattered at the same time. Barry had always been what she considered guarded in his speech, which she felt was one of the reasons he was in the position he was in. For his part, he knew he had stepped over the line, but he was glad he said it the way he did because he had thought it that way many times.

"So how far along are you?"

"Not very far. A little over two months."

"You can still change your mind, you know."

"Yes, I know, but I won't."

CHAPTER TEN

She had three voicemails from Teddy by the time she got to her office at 11:00. She knew what they were about, and she didn't listen to them. She texted him that she was in her office and wanted to speak to him in person.

Rene could still hear Barry reminding her that she could change her mind, and telling her what she already knew—that if she didn't terminate the pregnancy, it was going to be exceedingly difficult for her to continue her career. She had told him she wouldn't change her mind, but it was all finally caving in on her.

She called her mother. No answer. On her own again. She knew this decision could change her life completely, and she had to admit something unusual for her—she still didn't have the answer.

Rene looked up and he was standing in the doorway. She stood up. Neither one of them said a word. He walked around her desk and wrapped his arms tight around her.

"I'm here regardless of what you decide," he said as he kissed her.

That was not at all what she had expected him to say. Was he saying if she terminated the pregnancy, he would stay with her? That was something she hadn't included in the possible scenarios, and only made things more difficult. Would she feel obligated to marry him in return even though there was no child? She was having to come to terms with the fact that he might really be in love with her even if she weren't pregnant.

And what were her feelings for him? Was she falling for him or were all the events swirling around her making her want support from anyone involved in the drama? Whether she was in love with him or not, she knew she had to decide.

"I'm keeping the baby." It was the first time she'd called it a baby.

"I want you to want it the way I do."

"I can't tell you that. I'm only saying I'm not terminating the pregnancy and I'm going to need all the help I can get from you and everybody else."

CHAPTER ELEVEN

She was in Gerry's office for her checkup. Everything looked good, which surprised even him considering her age. He had told her a couple weeks earlier that it was a girl, which both she and Teddy seemed very happy about. She said she found Teddy already looking at the baby names book.

"You really could have given me a heads up on this, Gerry. This is hard enough as it is, as you well know."

"It never crossed my mind, Rene."

"Would that be because you're a man?"

"You know that's really not fair. I've been more than supportive from the beginning."

"I want sex for breakfast, lunch, and dinner, which makes everything more difficult. Nobody told me the second trimester made that happen."

"I'm sure Teddy's happy."

"It's certainly the last thing he expected. And the last thing I expected."

"At his age, I'm sure he's having no trouble accommodating you."

"That's not the point, is it? To say we both have demanding careers is obviously an understatement."

"I imagine at this point you've found all the broom closets."

"That's really not funny."

"Lighten up, Rene. You're doing something beautiful that you never expected, and as a sidebar, nature is forcing some physical pleasure on you. What's to object to? I'm sure this is the result of nature wanting the dinosaur slayers to stay near the pregnant cave women. You're not married to him, and you say you still don't know how you feel about him, so find a pinch hitter. You have plenty of men on your dance card."

"In case you've forgotten, I'm pregnant."

"Nobody knows that unless you tell them. You're not showing yet. It's the perfect birth control."

"That's disgusting."

"Maybe so, but it's a fact, so use it if you need to."

CHAPTER TWELVE

"Hi, Sonny, glad you called. You were on my list. Sorry I missed last week. My schedule got away from me. Yes, tomorrow would be great. Same time? Good idea. Yes, bring a roast chicken. Yes, really looking forward to it. Missed you, too."

She already knew this was probably a mistake, because she really did have strong feelings for Teddy, but Gerry was right that she hadn't married him. She wanted to stay independent in part because she had never anticipated being pregnant, and this rendezvous was clearly a reflection of those feelings.

He appeared at her door on time as usual. Jake was with Faye, so there was no problem there. Faye knew what Rene's dinner engagements were about because she changed the sheets. He handed her the chicken and kissed her. He could tell she was already turned on from her kiss, which was deep and sensuous.

"Whatever you want."

She put her arms around his neck. "Nothing fancy. Just a lot."

She dropped the chicken on the kitchen counter. They kissed again as they walked to the bedroom, undressed each other, and fell into bed. He didn't know why she was already turned on, but he didn't care. She knew. She came twice and then again.

"Can you stay?"

"Yes." She'd never asked him to do that before.

"Do you have call?"

"Yes, but I'll work it out." He didn't know what his feelings were for her, but they were definitely more than sexual, which he wasn't ready for. She was so much in control in her work, but seemed so vulnerable in bed, which he found incredibly attractive. He actually felt protective of her, which was the last thing he'd expected. He could feel his touch change, although he didn't know whether she could.

"Hungry?"

"Yes, very."

"I'll get us some chicken. White meat or dark?

"Doesn't matter."

She watched him walk naked out to the kitchen the way she thought a man would watch a beautiful woman. She had always been attracted to fair haired men, but he was clearly the exception. If there was such a thing as a beautiful man, he was it. Tall, with broad shoulders, a slim waist, and a perfect ass. She wondered whether he got his good looks from his mother or father or both.

He came back in a few with a plate of chicken, some grapes, and some sparkling water. She struggled to look at the food. He had a perfect uncircumcised penis. She wondered how that had happened. She also wondered how many American women had actually seen one.

"Were you born at home?"

"How did you know?"

"Just guessing."

He put the plate down on the bed between them and got under the sheet. Thank goodness. She was hungry as she often was now and needed to concentrate on eating.

She knew sex wasn't always great on a full stomach, but she didn't care. He put the plate and the glasses on the floor. He could tell from the way she touched him that she wanted him again, and he obliged. The sex was clearly explosive for her, which he wanted to take full credit for, but wasn't sure he could. He had had many testimonials regarding his sexual prowess, but knew from experience that something else was going on with her.

He took his clothes to the kitchen so he wouldn't wake her up dressing. She had rounds in the afternoon, but nothing scheduled in the morning. He set the clock for 8:00, although he knew her work made her an early riser. He brushed back her hair and kissed her on the forehead. She turned and kept sleeping. He didn't know what was happening, but he knew something had changed.

CHAPTER THIRTEEN

"**S**onny, I need to see you in my office. When can you come by? 2:00? Great. See you then."

She knew she'd made a big mistake sleeping with him the week before and felt she owed it to him to be honest about the pregnancy before they were set to get together again. She sensed that he might be developing feelings for her, and it wasn't fair to him to let that go any further. He had been almost tender with her during their previous encounter. She was also more than a little apprehensive about the fact that she might be starting to care for him, and she needed to get those feelings under control as quickly as she could.

It had been a grueling week for her with several complex evaluations and surgeries, but she was holding up better than she had expected and thought this shouldn't wait. She had always made every effort to ensure that her personal life didn't impinge on her work, and she knew things were going to get harder if she didn't get control now.

"Hi, beautiful."

"Don't."

"Sorry, hello Dr. James."

He sat down in one of the chairs in front of her desk.

"Sonny, I need to tell you something I should have told you last week. I'm pregnant."

"Is it mine?"

"No, it's not."

"And you knew that when you fucked me."

"Yes."

"Do you know how shitty that is?"

"Yes."

"So why the hell did you do it?"

"Because I wanted you."

"Do you want me now?"

She paused. "Yes."

He walked over to the door and locked it. He came around the desk, picked her up and put her on the conference table. He pulled her to the edge, took down her pants, dropped his trousers and fucked her hard until they both came.

"Will that do it?" he said, pulling up his pants.

"Yes, definitely."

CHAPTER FOURTEEN

"I've told my parents about you and they're anxious to meet you," said Teddy. "I've told them you're brilliant and beautiful. No pressure."

"Did you happen to tell them how old I am? How old is your mother, by the way?"

"She's older than you are."

"Not by much, I'm sure. How did you explain me?"

"I told them we were very attracted to each other and that it happened unexpectedly."

"That's an understatement."

"I told them you had struggled with whether to keep the baby. I said that I had tried to convince you to keep it, and that you finally had. They seemed happy with that."

I guess I'll have a chance to decide for myself whether they are happy about the baby, she thought.

They were staying at the nicest hotel in town, which had a lobby bar where they were meeting. The bar was old and elegant. She had suggested a public place in case things didn't go well, although she didn't tell him that. She was aware they had money, although she'd never asked him directly and he'd never volunteered the information. She knew his father had a successful business and that his mother dabbled in interior design. She was glad they were not meeting at his apartment, which she was sure would have made her uncomfortable. She asked him if there was anything particular she needed to be aware of, but he was no help in that regard. It was unusual for her to feel ill at ease in social situations, but this was obviously different.

"Mom and Dad, this is Rene. I've already told you a lot about her. She's been a plastic surgeon for many years now."

She wished he wouldn't have mentioned the many years.

"Hello, dear, it's so nice to finally meet you. Teddy has only said wonderful things about you."

"It's great to meet both of you, too, Mrs. Ryan. You have a terrific son."

She could see where he got his good looks and his taste in clothes. They were right out of *Town and Country*. His mother was wearing a beautiful suit that was understated but obviously expensive. Her blond hair was swept back and soft. His father had on a sport coat that was clearly tailored for him and fit like a glove.

"Oh, please call me Leslie, and this is Ted."

So he's a junior, she thought. She couldn't help being amused at thinking how she fit into the family tradition, whatever that was. Teddy had been relatively mum on his family, obviously waiting to see how his parents reacted to her.

"How was your trip?"

49

"The flight was smooth as silk," his father replied. "We hardly ever have a bad experience with Delta."

Well-traveled, as she would have expected.

"Sit down, dear. What would you like to drink?"

The "dear" made her feel like a prospective daughter-in-law, even though they were the same age. She had no idea what he'd told them about their getting married.

"Sparkling water with lime would be great."

His father ordered McCallan neat, and his mother ordered Jack and Coke. A blue-collar drink for an upper-class woman, which she found made her much more interesting. She had no idea what Teddy drank. She'd slept with him, but never had a drink with him.

"Do you carry Nearest? If so, I'd like one with a splash." So he did have a life outside medicine, she thought.

"How are you feeling? You look lovely." said his mother.

The compliment was unexpected. She had the urge to say, "You, too," but felt it would seem solicited. She didn't look pregnant yet, although her clothes were getting tight around the waist.

"Thank you. I'm feeling much better than I thought I would. My doctor said my last checkup was absolutely normal, which he really hadn't expected because of my age." There, she'd confronted the elephant in the room. She detected the relief in his mother's face.

"I had Teddy when I was in my mid-20s. It was an easy pregnancy and delivery. I don't know why it would be any different for you if everything is normal."

"I'm counting on you being right. I'm planning on continuing working until the baby comes."

"That's a physically demanding job you've got there from what I understand," his father said, furrowing his brow. "You might want to reconsider."

"I wouldn't have kept the baby if I hadn't thought I could keep working. My work is very important to me."

"Rene and I have discussed it. She'll have help from lots of people, including me."

"But you have a very demanding career, too, and a very busy work schedule."

"Ted, we can discuss this later. How's your drink?"

"Great. So, are you planning to get married?" She let Teddy take that one. She knew it was coming.

"I've asked Rene to marry me, but we haven't decided yet."

"You mean she hasn't decided yet. So, Rene, what's the holdup?"

"Well, for starters, I thought you would object because of the age difference. Leslie, you and I are the same age. I also thought that this time in his career was a problem. He has a promising one. Obviously, neither one of us planned this."

"Do you love him?" his mother asked. "He says he loves you."

"Yes." She had never said it before.

Teddy turned and looked straight at her. She smiled. He walked over and put his arm around her shoulders.

"So pick a date. Leslie, at the house. A few people."

She was totally taken aback by his enthusiasm. Now she had another decision to make.

CHAPTER FIFTEEN

The goodbyes had been cordial with Teddy promising to look for a date for the wedding. Rene smiled but didn't make any promises. They walked out of the lobby to the valet station. Teddy handed the valet the ticket.

"So did you mean it or was it just for them?"

"We can talk about it in the car."

Not a good sign, he thought. The valet brought his car up. Teddy tipped him and they got in. He pulled up a few feet and stopped.

"So, what's the answer?"

"Yes, I meant it."

"Look at me and say it."

She looked straight at him. "Okay, I don't know how I got here, but, yes, I'm in love with you."

He leaned across the console and gave her a passionate kiss. He heard a knock on his window. It was the valet. He lowered the window.

"Sorry."

"Hey, man, I get it. She's hot. Just pull up some."

"Sure," he said as he closed the window and pulled up.

She couldn't contain herself. "Fifty-two, pregnant, and hot?"

"Hey, if the valet says you're hot, you're hot." He kissed her again.

"You know I have several reasons right now to take you home and fuck your lights out."

He surprised her. That wasn't his usual language, but she'd just told him she was in love with him and she wanted him, too.

"Yes, my house is fine." She put her hand on his thigh.

"I'm starving." They were halfway to her house.

"Geez, Rene, I forgot. Will pizza do?"

"Only if it has everything."

He called and ordered from their favorite place. It would be there just about when they arrived. They drove up to her house just as the pizza arrived. He tipped the delivery driver and took it in. It was still hot. She opened the box and took out a piece before he could get the plates. He felt bad about forgetting how hungry she got because she was pregnant. She finished her second piece just as he started on his first.

"You know, I want you almost as much as this pizza. I'm hoping you have everything for me, too." She had always been ironically funny. It was one of the things he loved about her. She was still in sexual overdrive, and she had finally admitted to herself that she'd actually fallen for this guy. "Done." She had eaten almost the entire pizza. "So, I'm ready for everything you've got."

He'd been in love with her for a while now, and they'd always had great sex, but this was the first time he'd slept with her since she'd said she was in love with him, so he wanted it to be as good as he could make it. She started undressing him on the way to the bedroom, so he knew she wasn't lying about really wanting him.

They were both ready when they fell into bed. She'd never thought much about the term "turned on," but now she was feeling what she sensed was almost an electrical charge on her skin when he touched her. He went deep inside her and she felt every inch. She had always heard that sex was really in the brain. She had slept with him before and it had been good, but never like this. She must have released something in her body when she admitted she was in love with him.

"Oh, Teddy, what's happening?"

"Not sure, but I don't want it to stop," he said, going even deeper.

"Don't make me come yet. I want this to last." He tried to slow down but couldn't. They both came in an orgasm that seemed to last forever.

CHAPTER SIXTEEN

Rene always looked stylish and elegant at public events, but it was the little quirks Teddy learned about when he began living with her that made him fall even more in love with her. For example, she almost always wore socks to bed. She had been anemic at some point, which had given her cold feet, but long after the anemia was a thing of the past, she still wore socks to bed. He was regularly amused by the sight of her, beautiful and naked, walking around in fuzzy socks. He was grateful, however, for the fact that she always took her socks off when she wanted him, because he always wanted her.

He also learned that she didn't like the various food items on her plate to touch each other, something most kids grow out of by the age of five. It dawned on him that that was why she seldom ate much at banquets, even when he knew she had to be hungry. He now often called ahead with a request for her, and they always gladly complied. That meant she ate her dinners, which was particularly important now that she was pregnant.

He was electronically gifted. In fact, he had been advised to start his own technology company instead of going to medical school, but that wasn't his vision for himself. He had figured out how to program the stereo system in her car to play a love song he'd picked out for her every morning when she started her car. It took a while for her to figure out what was going on, but when she finally did, she thought it was hilarious.

That evening, they had ordered Chinese. They were sitting at the table in the kitchen, and she was eating her lo mein. She pointed her chopsticks at him.

"So, is it true?"

"Is what true?"

"That you only have eyes for me?"

He looked surprised and then laughed. He had put *I Only Have Eyes for You* on her stereo for that morning.

"Busted."

"How do you do it?"

"Not talking."

She stood up, walked around the table and kissed him.

"Don't stop."

He put her to bed early with a kiss, as he had been doing for a while. She was keeping up her grueling schedule, but he knew she had to be tired. He had been sleeping in the guest room because she often slept in the nude now, and it was very difficult for him to keep his hands off her.

He didn't know what time it was, except that it was the middle of the night. He felt her slip into bed behind him, press her belly into the small of his back and kiss him on the neck. He turned and kissed her on the mouth.

"I'm sorry, but I really want you right now," she whispered.

Sex was easier now from the back, but he wanted to look at her when he was making love to her. And so he braced himself on his arms over her belly and looked right at her. She knew he was paying attention, so she talked to him about what she wanted, which made the sex even more erotic. It also allowed him to time his orgasm to hers. He held her almost like a child as she went to sleep.

It had never occurred to him that pregnant sex would be so good, but he was certainly happy that it was. They had asked Gerry when they should stop having sex, and he had said when the baby's head was crowning, which had made them both laugh. It had also freed him up to give her what she wanted.

CHAPTER SEVENTEEN

Her cellphone rang. She turned on her pillow. The phone showed 2:15 and the name of the chief's assistant, Denise.

"This is Rene. Denise, what's going on?"

"Oh, my God! When?" Barry had had a heart attack a couple hours earlier and was in Intensive Care at University Hospital.

"Should I come? Where is Alice? How is she?" She liked Alice very much. "I'd like to be there for her. Okay, I'm leaving as soon as I can get dressed."

Teddy was waking up, and she filled him in on what had happened.

"I'm going to the hospital to be with Alice."

"I'll drive you."

She was happy to accept his offer. She was tired, and he knew it.

The hospital was 20 minutes away. They made it in 15. They parked in Visitor Parking and went immediately to the Intensive Care area. She had her hospital credentials, which got them into the family waiting area. Alice was there sitting by herself. Rene went over and put her arms around her.

"Oh, Alice, I can't believe it. How is he doing? How are you doing? What can I get you? Have you eaten anything?"

"He'd had some heart trouble years ago, but was on medication and had not had any symptoms for a long time. But he'd been under a lot of stress recently."

She hoped she hadn't been part of that. She got them both a cup of coffee and a bag of cookies out of the vending machine. She knew they had two children who lived out of town, one in New York and one in Atlanta.

"Are the kids coming? They must be in shock."

"Yes, disbelief is probably a better word. They should be here in a couple hours."

"Is there anything we need to take care of at the house? Teddy can feed the dogs and let them out." She had been to their house and knew they had two dogs.

"That would be great. I don't know how long I'm going to be here."

Just as she spoke, a doctor came out. He had an indecipherable look on his face that he had probably practiced.

"We tried everything, Mrs. Ross, but he didn't make it."

Alice froze. After a minute, she said, "I want to see him."

"Of course. Please come with me."

Rene let go of Alice's hand and watched her go into the emergency room. She was a small woman and looked even smaller as she walked away.

When she came out, Rene walked up to her and said, "You're staying with us tonight." Alice didn't object. Teddy went to bring the car around. Rene got in the back seat with Alice and put her arm around her. Alice stared out the window. When they got to the house, Rene got Alice a pair of her pajamas and helped her into them. She put her into their bed and got in with her. She wasn't going to leave her alone.

CHAPTER EIGHTEEN

Rene woke up the next morning early. Alice was still sleeping, and Teddy was in the guest room with Jake. Alice's children had called, and she had told them their mother was staying with them. She had rounds but had no idea what else was going on. She called Denise for an update.

"Hi, Denise, what's the latest? Yes, we're all in shock. Alice is at my house and still asleep. I'm planning to make rounds as usual. Anything I need to know? You're kidding."

Denise said the Board had made Mark Browning the interim chief. Browning was her immediate supervisor and had made it his mission for years to undermine her. Her colleagues had told her he was jealous of her skill and the fact that she was so well known. She also knew that he wanted to sleep with her. This clearly was not good news for her.

Mark was sitting behind Barry's desk. He had asked her to meet with him.

"Hello, Rene. How are you feeling this morning?"

"Great, as usual."

"No morning sickness?"

"Nope. Never had any. How are you liking your new job?" She knew he was loving every minute of it.

"Listen, I understand that the father of this baby is Teddy Ryan, who is one of our residents."

"That's correct."

"If I'm not mistaken, you are one of his supervisors."

"Technically, yes, although, as you know, he's not in our department."

"I'm sure you know that's a violation of University policy."

She didn't respond.

"He's going to have to find a residency at some other institution."

"You must be kidding."

"That's the rule, unless, of course, we can find another solution."

"And what would that be?"

He reached in his pocket, took out a hotel room key and handed it to her.

"I'm pregnant."

"Do you really think I give a shit? Do you have any idea how long I've wanted to fuck you?"

Actually, she did.

"Tonight at 9:00. See you then."

"How do I know you'll keep your word?"

"It depends on how good the fuck is. Your reputation precedes you."

CHAPTER NINETEEN

She told Teddy she was meeting an old college friend and would probably be late. She knocked on the hotel room door exactly at 9:00. He opened the door. He was already wearing the hotel robe. She had prepared for this by imagining how she would visualize Teddy in his place but had no idea whether it would actually work. She knew she was going to be eligible for an Academy Award when it was all over.

"Hello, Rene, right on time, as usual."

"Always." Even for you, she thought.

He opened the door wider and she stepped in. He took her face in his hands and kissed her. She knew she had to kiss him back, and she did. He unbuttoned her blouse and unclasped her bra. Her breasts were full and beautiful, and she let him have them. He took them in his mouth one at a time and sucked them. She knew, however, that this was just the beginning.

He pulled down her pants. She had no underwear on. Why bother when she knew what was going to happen. He backed her over to the bed and pushed himself inside her.

"Shit. Rene, do you know how long I've wanted to do this?"

"Yes, from the beginning."

"Yes."

He moved faster and faster inside her until he came. She said Teddy's name to herself with every thrust.

He was still hard. "Suck me."

She went down under the sheet and gave him the best blow job she knew how. She even swallowed. She kept thinking about his comment: "Depends on how good the fuck is."

"Christ, Rene, were they right," he said when she came up. He kissed her.

He was hard enough to go inside her again. It was difficult for her to imagine how turned on he was. He came again and kissed her again.

"Are you feeling okay? Are you satisfied?" As if he cared, she thought.

"Yes, although I have rounds tomorrow morning and I really should get home."

"I understand completely. Let me help you."

She couldn't believe he was helping her get dressed.

"You were spectacular." He kissed her goodbye.

She knew the Academy Award would be waiting for her at her front door.

It was 11:30 when she got home. She walked down the hall to the bathroom and threw up. Teddy came in with Jake close behind him. She had never been sick during her pregnancy and Teddy was worried.

"It's okay, boy," she said, patting Jake's head. Jake was very protective of her.

"Are you alright, Baby?"

"Yes," she said, wiping her mouth with a tissue. "I just need a shower."

He didn't ask any questions. He helped her undress, adjusted the water temperature in the shower and helped her in.

"I'll get some fresh towels."

"Thanks, that would be good."

Teddy took Jake out with him.

She washed every part of her she could reach. She needed to wash Browning completely off of her.

"Teddy, would you wash my back?" she asked when he came back in with the towels. She didn't tell him why. She didn't want him to feel responsible for any of it.

"Of course." He took off his boxers, got into the shower and washed her back. When he was finished, she turned around and faced him.

"Hold me." He put his arms around her. She was trembling. They stood under the water until the trembling stopped. He turned off the water and dried her off with one of the towels. He took her robe off the hook in the bathroom and put it around her. He walked her down the hall to the bedroom and got into bed with her.

"I'm here and I'm not going anywhere."

He put his arms around her and she kissed him. He didn't know what was going on, but he didn't care. He was very much in love with her.

CHAPTER TWENTY

Denise was sitting at her desk outside Browning's office. Rene strode past her without saying a word and burst into Browning office. She heard Rene say, "You son of a bitch," before the door slammed shut.

"How are you this morning, Rene?"

"You damned well know how I am. Teddy isn't on the assignment list."

"We discussed this earlier, Rene. It's a violation of University policy for you to supervise him."

"You bastard. What the fuck did you think I was sucking your dick for last night? I gave you everything I had."

"As a matter of fact, you were so good last night, I almost changed my mind. I don't know where you learned to move like that, and I must admit the blow job was spectacular. But I want this job to be permanent, and not making Teddy leave would definitely be questioned by those making that decision."

"If you knew that last night, why didn't you tell me?"

"Then I wouldn't have gotten the best blow job I ever got. You really are magic in the sack."

"Where did you hear that?"

"When I said your reputation precedes you, I wasn't kidding. And they were right. We all know you're no virgin. Your belly betrays that. Of course, if you want to be the one to leave, feel free."

"Are you kidding? You must know they'd never let me go. I'm the prize pony. Nobody else does the operations I do."

"Yes, I'm well aware that my efforts to marginalize you have always been futile. You're too talented, and I must add, too beautiful. You confirmed that last night, even five months pregnant."

"I guess that was meant to be a compliment. It makes me want to throw up, which, by the way, I did last night."

"Oh, come on, Rene, you know you enjoyed yourself. That couldn't have all been faked."

"You are too easily fooled."

"How often do you do that for the boy?"

"None of your damned business. I've got to finish my rounds."

"Lucky bastard." He said as she slammed the door behind her.

CHAPTER TWENTY-ONE

The minute she finished her rounds, she called Marilyn. She had met Marilyn at a cocktail party several years ago. A mutual friend had introduced them. Her friend said Rene was having trouble with her supervisor and really needed to speak with a lawyer.

Marilyn met with Rene the next day, and after finding out what was going on in her department, came up with a strategy that would allow her to obtain a comparable position at another major university.

Problem solved, although Marilyn knew from her many years of practice that she would, in all likelihood, be hearing from Rene again. Men weren't going to change, and Rene was just too smart and beautiful.

"Hello, Marilyn. This is Rene. Yes, it's definitely been a while. As you predicted, different park, same trailer."

Marilyn laughed. "It's good to hear from you again. So what's going on up there? Something interesting, I'm sure."

Rene gave her a detailed account of her current situation.

"Geez, Rene, I didn't think it would be that interesting. How old are you now? And you're five months pregnant, so you've decided to keep the baby. And the father, Teddy, is how old? He says he wants to marry you, but how about you? And the new interim chief says you can't supervise Teddy, so he has to leave. But the chief then promised you that if you slept with him, which you did, Teddy could stay. But now, he's gone back on his promise, and Teddy has to go. So now you want to sue him and the university for sex discrimination and harassment. Have I got that all right?"

"Yes."

"You know, I told you years ago that if you sued the university, you'd never find another academic position. Do you remember that? Because it's still true. Are you ready for that? Because you probably have another 15 years left on what I understand can only be described as an illustrious career. Can't you just find the kid another residency once you cool off? There's another good university just up the street."

"No. I've put up with this for years, and this time, I've just had it."

"Is that because of him, or are you just fed up?"

"Both."

"Are you in love with him, because if you are, you can't let that interfere with this decision, which clearly will have such a significant impact on your career."

Rene did not respond. "Isn't there an anti-retaliation provision in the law?"

"Yes, but I always tell my clients that it isn't what happened that matters, but what you can prove. You'd have to prove that you slept with the guy because he promised to violate a university rule if you did, but he decided not to. That's a tough starting point."

"Isn't the bottom line that I wouldn't have slept with him otherwise?"

"Yes, the test is whether or not it was 'welcome.' But you need to know that they can bring up your entire sexual history to prove that it was. As I remember, you have a full sex life, as a beautiful woman like you should."

"You need to know that there are some issues there." Rene told her about the residents and the notepad.

"Well, I've never had that one before. How long did that go on? Two-and-a-half years? So, you've had sex with a dozen or so attractive guys? Not a bad plan. I'm jealous," she said with a smile. "And Teddy was one of them? And for some reason, we think menopause, your birth control didn't work? And for some reason, you didn't terminate the pregnancy? I'm sorry, but you're going to have to explain that one to me, Rene. You're in your 50's. What were you thinking?"

"I guess, deep down, I really must have wanted a child. I'd never seen it as a real possibility in light of my career and my lifestyle, but then there it was. Probably a couple mistakes on my part, but too late now. And Teddy wants the baby, although I'm not sure what his thinking is either. He says he's in love with me."

"Was he in love with you when you had sex with him?"

"I certainly wasn't in love with him. He was just an attractive guy who wanted to sleep with me."

"Are you now?"

"It took me a while to admit it, but yes."

"Well, as Laurel said to Hardy, 'This is another fine mess you've gotten me into.'"

CHAPTER TWENTY-TWO

Rene and Teddy were standing in the kitchen. He had just overheard Marilyn and Rene discussing the pros and cons of calling Sonny as a witness.

"So let me get this straight. You had sex with Sonny at your request after you knew you were pregnant, and the baby was mine." Teddy didn't yell, but she had never seen him as upset as he was.

"Yes."

"You had to know how pissed off that would make me if I found out."

"Yes."

"So why the hell did you do it?"

"I didn't think it was any of your business."

"That doesn't answer the question."

"I'm not your property, and I had the right to have sex with whomever I wanted. And I wanted him."

Teddy sat down. "Were you in love with him?"

"No."

"Were you in love with me?"

"I hadn't decided."

"Shit, Rene, it sounds like you were picking out a sofa."

"Look, you know I don't do relationships well. I never have. The thought of being tied to one person wasn't on my radar. I've always fucked whomever I wanted to fuck, and I wanted to fuck Sonny. Don't criticize me for that. I'm old enough to be your mother, dammit."

She knew she had said the wrong thing as soon as it came out of her mouth.

He stepped over to her and took her upper arm in his hand. "Don't ever play that card with me."

"I'm really sorry. I know that's a bad topic for us."

"You must know at this point that I don't give a shit about your age. I've proven that many times. What else do you want from me? I've given you a baby."

"I was afraid of you. At least afraid of my feelings for you. And for the baby. You know that I had never wanted a child. I felt trapped by my decision, and I was looking for an answer to that. I know now that he wasn't it. And I told him that."

"So you felt trapped by the fact that the baby was mine and you had no alternative to being with me." She could tell he was both hurt and angry.

"Yes, I felt that I wasn't in control of that decision anymore, and that scared me. But that's not the case anymore."

"So why would that be?"

"Because I really am in love with you, and I do want to be with you. Problem solved," she said with a smile.

"Is it? What if you decide tomorrow that I'm not the solution?"

"I obviously can't predict tomorrow. All this has proven that for real. All I know is that I'm big time in love with you right now."

She reached up and started to unbutton her shirt.

"What are you doing?"

"I'm getting undressed." She slipped out of her shirt, kicked off her shoes and stepped out of her pants. She was standing in front of him naked.

"Take a good look. I'm giving it to you right now if you want it."

He had always been incredibly attracted to her physically and she knew it. He put his arms around her, lifted her up and took her into the bedroom. She could tell from the way he touched her as they made love that he wasn't angry with her anymore. She reached up and touched his hair as they lay side by side. His hair was close-cropped and soft.

"I meant it, and I really do love you."

CHAPTER TWENTY-THREE

Marilyn had been handling these cases longer than Rene had been fixing children's faces and knew just what she needed to do. She wasn't as tall or striking as Rene, but she was well-dressed and attractive enough to make an impression. Expensive, understated suits and jewelry, medium-length blonde hair with touches of gray, bright blue eyes that sparkled when she was winning a point. Her pleasant, friendly demeanor made those who didn't know her think she might be a push-over, but those who had been up against her knew better. She always tried the case as if she were the plaintiff, and she was tough as nails. She sometimes wore glasses with clear lenses so she looked more imposing. Rene was unaware of how lucky she was to have found her. She would soon find out.

Rene was smart as a whip, but this area of the law was complicated, and Marilyn thought it was important for Rene to understand exactly what was going on. Marilyn took Rene to lunch at one of the places near the courthouse frequented by lawyers because of the quick service and good food.

"We have to file a Charge of Discrimination with the Equal Employment Opportunity Commission before we can file our lawsuit against the university under the federal law", Marilyn told Rene. "I'll prepare a Charge for your signature, and we'll walk it down to the EEOC's office."

Title VII of the 1964 Civil Rights Act, the federal law that prohibits discrimination on the basis of sex and pregnancy and also prohibits sexual harassment, requires that a charge be filed as a prerequisite to any lawsuit under the law.

"We also have to get the Commission to issue a Notice of Right to Sue before we can bring our action, which usually takes months. But I know the Director and the Commission's docket is full, so I think I can get the Notice issued quickly." Marilyn was right. The advantages of age and connections.

"We can't sue Browning under the federal law because it only applies to employers, and the university is considered the employer, so we'll have to sue him personally under state law and ask the federal court to exercise supplemental jurisdiction over him. The Court will do that because the state claims against Browning are directly related to the federal claims against the university".

"We'll sue Browning for assault and battery, which is any unwelcome touching, and for infliction of emotional distress. We'll also sued the university for negligent supervision of Browning, which is a state law claim, asserting that it should have monitored his conduct more carefully. Both the claims against the university and the claims against Browning are triable to a jury."

"Geez, Marilyn, I had no idea this was so complicated. How do you know all this?"

"Years of experience. It's how I earn the big bucks for both of us," Marilyn said laughing.

Marilyn prepared the complaint right away with the help of her paralegal, Wendy Thompson, and filed it immediately. The district had what was known as a "Rocket Docket," which meant the case would be tried quickly, something that was unusual for federal courts.

"If you think you can handle it, I want you to be pregnant for the trial and for the jury." Rene responded without hesitation that she could, although Marilyn wasn't sure she really understood how stressful the trial would be.

The trial was set for 60 days from the filing, which meant Rene would be almost eight months pregnant. Perfect. Marilyn and her staff would be ready.

Marilyn called Rene to tell her that they had drawn what she believed was the perfect judge for the case, Patricia Weldon. Judge Weldon had been appointed in 1991 by a moderate Republican President, George H.W. Bush. Unlike state court judges, who were elected, federal judges were all appointed for life, which was supposed to make them less influenced by politics. It also sometimes made them less responsive to societal change. That was not Judge Weldon.

Judge Weldon was smart, unbiased, and unflappable, which Marilyn thought would be good in a case that, by its nature, involved so much sex. She also had a good sense of humor. In fact, Marilyn thought from her cocktail interactions with the judge, that she might be happy to have a case that was clearly not boring. Like Marilyn, she had been a partner in one of the city's large law firms, so by definition, she understood the politics of sex discrimination and harassment and had learned how to navigate it. Both she and Marilyn had been savvy enough and attractive enough to survive it. Marilyn had also been offered a judgeship, but decided she wanted to finish her career suing the bastards instead. In making the decision, she was forced to admit to herself that she really loved practicing law.

Both Marilyn and Judge Weldon were divorced and had two children, a boy and a girl. All their children were doing well in good colleges, so that was not an issue for either of them. Their lives were the law, and they were both as good as you could get at it. Their children admired their achievements. It was going to be an interesting trial.

Judge Weldon's chambers, which were cavernous, sat behind the bench. They held her large office and three smaller offices, two for her law clerks who helped her research and write her opinions, and one for her docket clerk, who helped her manage the numerous cases she was assigned each year. There would be no opinion written in this case since the jury, not the judge, would make the final determination.

The walls of Judge Weldon's office were lined with beautiful books bound with leather and gold that were virtually never used in the computer era. There was a large conference table in the office surrounded by a dozen chairs with leather seats and backs that were surprisingly comfortable. She had chosen her big, beautiful desk from the warehouse that housed all the furniture from the retired judges. She was not a large woman, but she loved the desk so much, she really didn't care if it made her look smaller. She had already mused about whether she somehow might be able to keep it when she left the bench.

"The case will definitely draw the news media that followed university developments," Marilyn confided to Rene. Marilyn wanted Rene to be fully aware of the potential media circus. Judge Weldon also knew the case would be very likely to draw media coverage, and developed a plan for dealing with that, which she discussed with her law clerks and bailiffs, and with the attorneys for the parties. She had never allowed cameras in the courtroom and didn't plan to start now. Each news entity would receive one pass a day and the general public would be admitted on a first-come, first-served basis. She was sure the parties would want the witnesses sequestered, which meant they would not be allowed in the courtroom until the parties stated they would not be called or recalled.

CHAPTER TWENTY-FOUR

Marilyn continued her direct examination of Rene, which the jury seemed to be following with the interest Marilyn had hope for. "You have brought this action against the university and the Chief of Surgery claiming sexual harassment and sex discrimination. Would you please explain the basis of your claims to the jury?"

"Yes. Dr. Mark Browning, my former supervisor who recently was made the interim Chief of Surgery when his predecessor died of a heart attack, forced me to have sex with him by threatening to terminate Dr. Ryan's residency if I didn't. Dr. Ryan is the father of my baby and Dr. Browning knew that. I reported Dr. Browning' threats and conduct to the university Human Resources Department, but they took no action."

"Did you, in fact, have sex with Dr. Browning in an effort to protect Dr. Ryan's residency."

"Yes."

"Please tell the jury about that encounter."

"Dr. Browning called me into his office and told me that Dr. Ryan was going to have to find a residency someplace else since it was against university policy for me to supervise him. When I pointed out that I didn't actually supervise him since he wasn't in my department, and that the prior chief had had no objection, Browning said the policy was clear unless we could find another solution. When I asked him what that would be, he handed me a hotel room key.

"Your Honor, Plaintiff introduces Plaintiff's Exhibit 1, which is the Hyatt Hotel room key Dr. James has identified."

"Dr. James, I want you to tell the jury exactly what Dr. Browning said to you at that point."

"When I told Dr. Browning I was pregnant, he said 'Do you think I give a shit? Do you know how long I've wanted to fuck you?' I asked him how I would know he was going to keep his word, and he replied, 'It depends on how good the fuck is. Your reputation precedes you.'"

"Did you show up at the hotel that evening?"

"Yes, at 9:00, as Dr. Browning had told me to."

"What happened then? Please be specific with the details."

"I knocked. Dr. Browning came to the door in a hotel robe. I stepped in and he kissed me. He took off my blouse and my bra and sucked my breasts. He pulled down my pants and backed me onto the bed. He shoved his penis inside me and proceeded to have sex with me for what seemed like an eternity until he had an orgasm. He then told me to suck his penis, which I did, until he had another orgasm. His penis was still hard, so he went inside me one more time. When he was finished, he asked me how I was doing and if I was satisfied. I said I was fine, but that I had call the next morning and needed to go. He said I had been spectacular and actually helped me get dressed. I drove myself home, walked into the bathroom and threw up."

"Did anyone see you throw up?"

"Yes, Teddy Ryan, who is the baby's father and who is living with me. He came into the bathroom and asked if I was okay"

"Have you ever had morning sickness?"

"No, never, and Teddy knew that."

"What happened then?"

"I told Teddy I needed to take a shower. He helped me undress, adjusted the water temperature and helped me into the shower."

"Did you tell him anything about why you wanted a shower?"

"No, and he didn't ask. I washed everything I could reach. I wanted to get Browning completely off me. When Teddy came back in with some new towels, I asked him to wash my back. He took off his boxers, got into the shower, and washed my back. When he finished, I turned around and asked him to hold me. He did for several minutes. Then we got out of the shower, and he dried me off, walked me down the hall to the bedroom, and got into bed with me."

"Did you say anything to him about what had happened to you that night?"

"No, nothing, and he didn't ask."

"Please tell the jury what happened the next morning."

"I had just started my rounds when one of the nurses gave me a copy of the residents' assignment sheet. Teddy's name wasn't on it. I went immediately to Dr. Browning's office. I pushed the door open, called him a son-of-a-bitch, and slammed the door shut behind me. When I asked him why he had reneged on his promise, he said I had been really something the night before, but that he wanted his job permanently, and the Board would ask about Teddy. When I asked him why he hadn't told me that before, he replied that he would have missed out on the best oral sex he'd ever had."

"Did he use the term 'oral sex'?"

"No, he used the term 'blow job.'"

"So, what did you do then?"

"I finished my rounds and then called you."

"Would you have called me if Teddy had been on the list?"

"Yes, just not as fast."

"Did you make a complaint to the medical school's Human Resources Department about Dr. Browning's sexual harassment?"

"Yes, I made a complaint in person that afternoon to the assistant director."

"Your Honor, Plaintiff introduces the Kenton University Human Resources Manual as Plaintiff's Exhibit 2."

"Did you report to the Human Resources Assistant Director what you've testified to here today?"

"Yes, all of it."

"Did the university take any action with regard to your complaint?"

"No."

"No further questions, your Honor."

CHAPTER TWENTY-FIVE

Warren Kramer stood and began his cross examination of Rene. He was in his late 60s with white hair and still good looking. He was effective not because he was belligerent, but because he was smart and charming.

"Good afternoon, Dr. James."

"Good afternoon."

"My name is Warren Kramer, and I'm the attorney for the Defendants in this case."

"Yes, I know."

"Dr. James, help me understand the numbers here. If I've heard your testimony correctly, you had sexual relations with 15 residents in two-and-a-half years, am I right?"

"Actually, it was 16. I met an additional resident when he came to observe one of my operations."

"Thanks for the correction. Explain to me why you thought that was a good idea."

"Mr. Kramer, would you ask me that question if I were a man?"

Kramer smiled. "Dr. James, let me explain how this works. I ask the questions and you answer the questions."

He is charming, she thought. Watch yourself.

"I wanted these residents to understand from the beginning, both through what I explained to them and how our meetings were structured, that our relationships were not meant to be long-term. To let them believe otherwise certainly would not be fair to them or fair to me. I was substantially older than they were and never expected these relationships to have any permanency. And I let them know that in every way I could. But as I testified earlier, I wasn't planning to spend the rest of my life without men in it."

"But you were surrounded by men, were you not?"

"I've always thought it was a bad idea to have intimate personal relationships with superiors and coworkers. Those are the men I'm surrounded by."

"So, you don't consider these residents to be co-workers?"

"No."

"They worked in the University Hospital, did they not?"

"They were assigned to various departments in the hospital based on their areas of specialization. I made certain I never had relationships with any of the residents in my department."

"But you had authority over more than just your department, didn't you?"

"Technically, yes, but I never exercised it, and never had any reason to exercise it, as my prior chief knew."

"So, technically, if you had wanted to benefit Dr. Ryan in some way, you could have, am I correct?"

"I would have had no idea how to do that, and I would have found that completely improper, as my former chief knew. I would not have jeopardized my career to do something like that. Dr. Ryan is the father of my baby quite by accident, and I don't owe him that."

Pretty good answer, Marilyn thought.

"But Dr. Browning wasn't technically wrong in assessing it as against university policy for you to continue to have the authority to supervise Dr. Ryan, even if you decided not to exercise it, am I right?"

"Even if that were the case, Dr. Browning could have just terminated Dr. Ryan's residency without coercing me into having sex with him in order to protect it, when he had no intention of doing so."

That's the case right there. Good job, Rene, thought Marilyn. Nice to have a smart client.

"Did any of these residents tell you they were in love with you?"

Marilyn stood. "Your Honor, I'm going to object to the question as irrelevant."

"Sustained. Find another direction, Counsel."

"Dr. James, let me ask you about Dr. Ryan. He is the father of your baby, correct?"

"Yes."

"Has he told you that he's in love with you?"

"Yes."

"And has he asked you to marry him?"

"Yes."

"And what was your response?"

"I haven't given him one."

"But you care enough about him to want to protect his residency, am I right?"

"I care enough about him to not let his residency be compromised by someone using me to jeopardize him."

"And it's your assertion that the only reason you had sex with Dr. Browning was that you were trying to prevent him from terminating Dr. Ryan's residency."

'Yes, that's right."

"You've admitted to having sex with a number of men, have you not?"

"Yes."

"But you never considered having sex with Dr. Browning?"

"Absolutely not."

"You'll concede that Dr. Browning is an attractive man, and that he was interested in you sexually?"

"I'll concede that he was interested in me sexually. He made that clear on many occasions. With regard to attractiveness, he was my supervisor, so I made it a point not to view him in that way."

"But with regard to the residents, you were at least technically their supervisor and you have admitted viewing them in terms of their attractiveness, have you not?"

"I never asserted any supervisory authority over any of them."

"But you could have."

"But I never would have, and that's the question, isn't it? Dr. Browning's predecessor knew that and never questioned me."

"Let me ask you about the liaison you described with Dr. Browning."

"I wouldn't describe it as a 'liaison.' That implies that it was voluntary."

"So, it's your position that Dr. Browning coerced you into meeting him in the Hyatt hotel room for sex by threatening you with the termination of Dr. Ryan's residency, is that correct?"

"Yes, exactly."

"But Dr. Browning asserts, does he not, that you knew of his sexual interest in you, and that you wanted to meet with him at the hotel to congratulate him on his promotion."

"That's totally untrue."

"But it's true, isn't it, that Dr. Browning had the authority to terminate Dr. Ryan's residency without consulting you at all."

"Of course, that's why it was so important to me to do everything I could to keep him from doing that. He knew he had personal leverage over me for the first time, and he used it to get what he never would have been able to get otherwise. I made the mistake of believing him."

"So, you're saying Dr. Browning is lying."

"Yes."

"No further questions, your Honor."

CHAPTER TWENTY-SIX

"The Plaintiff calls Edward Ryan." Teddy took the witness stand. He was tall and well-built with regular features and Coke-bottle green eyes. The clerk swore him in.

"Dr. Ryan, would you please state your full name for the record."

"Edward Holbrook Ryan, Junior."

"Do you have a nickname?"

"Yes. Teddy."

"What is your profession?"

"I am a physician."

"Where did you go to medical school?"

"Vanderbilt University."

"When did you graduate from medical school?"

"Six years ago."

"What is your current position?"

"I was a resident at Kenton Medical School until recently, when my residency was terminated."

"Why was that?"

"The reason I was given was that I could not be supervised by Dr. James because I had a close personal relationship with her."

"And what is that relationship?"

"She's carrying my baby."

An interesting way to put it, Marilyn thought. For sure, establishing his relationship with the child and with her at the same time.

"Were you given any other reason?"

"No."

"So, nothing about your work performance?"

"No, I always received top evaluations."

"Did Dr. James ever supervise you in any way?"

"No, never. She was in Plastic and Reconstructive Surgery, and I was in Cardiothoracic Surgery. Two completely different areas."

"But she held a high-level position in the medical school, did she not?"

"Yes, but that did not give her supervisory authority over my daily activities. She was not a specialist in cardiothoracic surgery and could not instruct me or evaluate my job performance."

"How did you and Dr. James meet?"

"I went to observe one of her surgeries. She is known for her surgical skill."

"So how did you get together?"

"I approached her after the surgery to congratulate her on the result and asked her if she wanted to get something to eat.

She said she had ordered food to be delivered to her house and asked if I wanted to join her. I said yes."

"Did you spend the night?"

"Yes."

"Whose idea was that?"

"She asked me if I wanted to stay, and I said yes."

"Did you have sex?"

"Yes. As a matter of fact, I think that's the night the baby was conceived."

"Why do you think that?"

"The sex was intense."

Rene glanced down. Not the response Marilyn wanted about Rene's having intense sex with a guy she'd just met.

"Did you see Dr. James again?"

"Yes, we got together the following Thursday."

"At her house again?"

"Yes. I was already falling in love with her, and I wanted to see her as often as I could."

"Did you find that problematic, since she was so much older than you were?"

"She is beautiful, brilliant, and talented. Age was never a factor. I always felt when I was with her that I was in a store where I couldn't afford any of the merchandise."

Rene looked directly at him and smiled.

"When did she tell you she was pregnant and that the baby was yours?"

"About two-and-a-half months after we'd met."

"What was your reaction?"

"I was very happy, which she didn't understand. She told me to think about it. I told her there was nothing to think about because I was in love with her and it was my baby. She then told me she hadn't made up her mind on whether to keep the baby. When I said I wanted her to keep it, and that I wanted her to marry me, she said that wasn't the solution. She said it was her decision, and that she would let me know when she decided."

"How long after that did she tell you what she had decided to do?"

"About two weeks."

"What did she say?"

"She said she had been advised that keeping the baby would be very damaging to her career, but that she was going to keep it. She also said she was going to need all the help from me and everyone else that she could get."

"Are you and Dr. James now living together?"

"Yes, she has a large house, and I told her that I wanted to move in with her to keep an eye on her and the baby. She lived alone and thought that was a good idea."

"So, when did that happen?"

"Not long after she told me she was pregnant."

"Do you remember a night when she told you she was meeting an old college friend and would be home late?"

"Yes."

"Tell me what you remember about that night."

"It was about 11:30 when I heard the door to the garage open and her walk down the hall. I got up right away since I'd been expecting her. I went into the bathroom and saw her throwing up."

"Let me ask you, Dr. Ryan, had Dr. James ever had morning sickness?"

"No, never, and in any case, this was at night."

"So, what did you do next?'

"I went over to her, put my arm around her and asked her if she was okay. She said yes, but that she needed to take a shower. I helped her get undressed, adjusted the water temperature in the shower and helped her in. I told her I was going to get some fresh towels, and she said fine. When I came back, she asked me to wash her back. I took off my shorts, got in the shower with her and washed her back. When I was finished, she turned around and asked me to hold her. I put my arms around her, and she was trembling. I held her until the trembling stopped, helped her out of the shower and dried her off. I put her robe around her, walked her down to the bedroom and got in bed with her."

"Did you ask her what had happened that evening?"

"No. I thought if she wanted me to know, she'd tell me."

"Did she get up the next morning and go into the hospital as usual?"

"Yes."

"When did you learn that your residency was being terminated?"

"The next morning."

"Who told you?"

"My department head."

"Did he tell you why?"

"Yes, he told me that my close personal relationship with Dr. James created a conflict of interest that couldn't be resolved, since she technically had supervisory authority over me. When I told him she had never supervised me, he said the decision had been made, and that he would help me find another position."

"No further questions, your Honor."

CHAPTER TWENTY-SEVEN

Kramer asked Teddy, "So would it be fair to say, Dr. Ryan, that you are crazy about Dr. James."

Teddy looked straight at Rene. "I'm very much in love with her, if that's what you're asking."

"And it's true, isn't it, that you would do anything for her?"

"Yes, although I wouldn't lie for her, and she wouldn't want me to."

Smart guy, thought Rene. That's where he'd try to get you to go.

"So, your testimony is that you had sex with Dr. James the first night you met, is that correct?"

"Yes. Neither one of us had that in mind, but it happened."

"Did she initiate the sex?"

Marilyn stood and objected.

"Sustained. Move on, counsel."

"So, when did you see Dr. James again?"

"The next night she was available, which was Thursday."

"And every week after that?"

"Yes."

"As a resident, you were essentially still a student, isn't that right?"

"Not in the traditional sense, no. I was already a physician who was specializing in a particular field."

"But Dr. James was an associate professor, which implies of course that she was in a teaching position, does it not?"

"Technically, yes, but she didn't teach me."

"But she was clearly in a position of authority that was above you as a resident, was she not?"

"I guess you could say so, although she never exercised that authority over me or my situation."

"But Dr. Browning would not be wrong in assuming that she could have exercised it, was he?"

"I don't know, although I do know she never would have, and from what she's told me, her prior boss didn't think she would have, either.

"It's fair to say, isn't it, Dr. Ryan, that Dr. James having sex with you on a regular basis gave her a reason for wanting to protect your interests?"

"I don't know that that's true. She's a very ethical person, and she also wouldn't want to jeopardize her career in any way."

"Am I correct that you and Dr. James are not married to each other?"

"Yes."

"Did Dr. James ever tell you that she had had sex with Dr. Browning?"

"No, although I learned about it later in connection with this lawsuit."

"If it was so traumatic for her, why do you think she didn't tell you about it?"

"I think she didn't want to involve me."

"But you were involved, weren't you?"

"Not in any way I knew about, which is why I think she didn't tell me."

"Or it could be that she, in fact, voluntarily had sex with Dr. Browning and it didn't go well, couldn't it."

"I'm not sure how it could go so badly that it made her throw up."

"But it's a possibility, isn't it?"

"Not that I can see."

"It's true, isn't it, that you have asked Dr. James to marry you."

"Yes."

"But she hasn't said yes, has she?"

"No, she hasn't."

"Is that because she's still seeing other men?"

"No, I don't think so."

"Is she still seeing other men?"

"Not that I know of."

"So, you're the only man she's seeing right now?"

"Yes."

"And you're the father of her baby?"

"Yes."

"No further questions, your Honor."

CHAPTER TWENTY-EIGHT

"Plaintiff calls Denise Perkins." Denise took her seat in the witness stand and the clerk swore her in.

"Ms. Perkins, where are you employed?"

"Kenton University Medical School."

"What is your position?"

"I'm the Administrative Assistant to the Chief of Surgery."

"How long have you held that position?"

"Eleven years."

"Who is the Chief of Surgery?"

"Dr. Mark Browning is the Interim Chief of Surgery. His predecessor, Dr. Barry Ross, passed away of a heart attack about two months ago."

"Do you know Dr. Rene James?"

"Yes, very well. She has been on the faculty of the Medical School for seven years. She is a well-known facial reconstruction surgeon."

"How often does Dr. James come by the chief's office."

"Until recently, she came by about once a week."

"What was her demeanor when she came by?"

"She was always cordial and friendly. She always stopped by my desk to say hello and ask how I was doing."

"Was there a time recently when her demeanor was different?"

"Yes, I remember it because she was not her usual self."

"Tell us about that. When was it?"

"I remember it was the day the resident assignments came out. I had typed the list out for Dr. Browning and emailed it to everyone in the various surgery departments."

"Was Dr. James one of the recipients?"

"Yes."

"Did she come by your desk that morning?"

"Yes.

"Did she stop to say hello?"

"No, she stormed past my desk and pushed Dr. Browning's door open without knocking. She said, 'You son-of-a-bitch,' and slammed the door behind her."

"Was it your observation that Dr. James was angry?"

"Yes, very."

"How long did she stay in Dr. Browning's office?"

"Not long. About five minutes. She slammed the door again as she left."

"Do you know what Dr. James was angry about?"

"No, although I assumed it had something to do with the resident assignment sheet."

"No further questions, your Honor."

Kramer stood up. "Ms. Perkins, my name is Warren Kramer, and I'm the attorney for the University Defendants. Let me ask you, Ms. Perkins, you don't know what Dr. James was angry about when she came past your desk on the morning you described, do you?"

"No."

"No further questions, your Honor."

CHAPTER TWENTY-NINE

"**P**laintiff calls Anthony Mastrangelo." Sonny took the witness stand and the witness oath.

"Please state your full name for the record."

"Anthony Joseph Mastrangelo. M-A-S-T-R-A-N-G-E-L-O." The court reporter nodded and smiled.

"What is your profession?"

"I'm a doctor."

"Where did you go to medical school?"

"The University of Miami. I wanted to get as far away from the Chicago cold as I could."

The jury smiled.

"When did you graduate?"

"Six years ago."

"Do you have a specialty?"

"Yes, gastroenterology."

"Do you know Dr. Rene James?"

"Yes."

"How did you meet Dr. James?"

"She came to introduce herself to the new residents. I understand that the medical school asked her to because she is a well-known surgeon."

"Did she speak to you?"

"Yes. She introduced herself and asked me where I was from. We talked for a few minutes, and she handed me a small note with her name and telephone number and the word 'Dinner' on it. She said, 'Let me know,' and walked on."

"Did you call her?"

"Yes. I thought it was a chance to get to know a faculty member. Plus, I'm Italian and she is a beautiful woman." The jury smiled.

"Did you feel any pressure to call her?"

"No, not at all. I felt I could have just ignored the note."

"When you called, did you and she decide on a time and place?"

"Yes, we decided to meet at her house on Wednesday at 8:00."

"Then what happened."

"I took her a nice bottle of Italian wine. We ended up having sex and then dinner."

"In that order?"

"Yes, I wanted her more than I wanted lasagna." The jury laughed.

"How often did you and Dr. James meet after that?"

"About a half dozen times."

"Did you feel pressured by her at any time to meet with her?"

"No. I met with her because I wanted to."

"No further questions, your Honor."

Warren Kramer stood up.

"Dr. Mastrangelo, did you and Dr. James have sex each time you got together?"

Marilyn objected.

"Sustained. Move on, counsel."

"Do you have feelings for Dr. James?"

"Yes."

"Are you in love with her?"

"Yes."

Holy shit, news to me, thought Marilyn, looking at Rene. How many of these guys fell for her?

"So, Dr. James' theory that the residents she saw on a temporary basis wouldn't develop a more permanent interest in her certainly didn't apply to you, did it?"

"No, she was wrong there. She doesn't look her age, and I think from her prior experiences with men her age, she doesn't realize how attractive she is."

Marilyn followed up, as she had to. "One more question, your Honor. Dr. Mastrangelo, would your feelings for Dr. James affect the truthfulness of your testimony?"

"Absolutely not."

"No further questions, your Honor."

DOUBLE STANDARD

CHAPTER THIRTY

"Your Honor, defendants call Dr. Mark Browning."

Dr. Browning took the stand.

"Do you swear to tell the truth, the whole truth and nothing but the truth?"

"I do."

"Dr. Browning, are you an individual defendant in this action?"

"Yes."

"And you have been at the counsel table and heard all the testimony in this action so far?"

"Yes."

"Dr. Browning, what is your profession?"

"I'm a physician and the Interim Chief of Surgery at Kenton Medical School"

"How long have you held that position?"

"Since the death of the previous Chief, Barry Ross, around two months ago."

"What was your position before that?"

"I was the Head of the Plastic and Reconstructive Surgery Department."

"Is Dr. Rene James in that department?"

"Yes, she is an associate professor in that department."

"How long has Dr. James held that position?"

"Around seven years."

"Have you been the head of the department for the entire time Dr. James has been in the department?"

"Yes."

"Dr. James' claim against you in this case is that you forced her to have sex with you in an attempt to keep you from terminating the residency of the father of her child, but that you terminated his residency anyway, is that your understanding?"

"Yes".

"Did you, in fact, have sex with Dr. James?"

"Yes, but there was nothing forced about it."

"Please explain."

"I had been attracted to Dr. James for some time. She is a very attractive woman. But she has always had a hard and fast rule that she would never have an intimate personal relationship with her immediate supervisor, and I respected that. But when Dr. Ross unexpectedly passed away, and I became the Chief of Surgery, I was no longer her immediate supervisor, and it was like the valve came off the pressure cooker. She let me know that she was open to an intimate encounter and suggested that she wanted to congratulate me on my promotion by meeting me for a night at the Hyatt. I, of course, agreed."

"Did you and Dr. James meet at the Hyatt?"

"Yes."

"And did you have sex?"

"Yes, pretty much as she has described, except that it was all voluntary on her part."

"Did she spend the entire night?"

"No, she said after an hour or so that she wasn't feeling well and thought she ought to go home. I helped her get dressed, told her she had been terrific and asked if I could drive her home. She said, no, that she felt well enough to drive herself and that she would see me in the morning."

"Did you, in fact, see Dr. James the next morning?"

"Yes, she came to my office angry about the fact that Dr. Ryan was not on the resident assignment list, which had come out that morning."

"Was that your decision?"

"Yes, and Dr. James knew it was an issue because of her obvious personal relationship with him and the fact that she was in a supervisory position over him. It was something we had discussed. I had told her he was going to have to find a residency at another university, but for whatever reason, she apparently didn't believe me."

"Did her having sex with you have any impact to your decision?"

"No, obviously not."

"No further questions, your Honor."

Marilyn stood and began her cross of Dr. Browning.

"So, Dr. Browning, you admit that you had wanted to have sex with Dr. James for some time, am I correct?"

"Yes."

"But that she only agreed after you became Interim Chief of Surgery and you were no longer her immediate supervisor, am I right?"

"Yes, that's correct."

"But that's not a permanent position for you, is it?"

"No."

"So, if someone else is chosen to permanently fill that position, you would return to your position as Dr. James' immediate supervisor, am I correct?"

"Yes."

"And Dr. James is a smart enough woman to know that, isn't she?"

"I presume so."

"So, you're claiming that she approached you about having a sexual encounter with her knowing that you might at any time become her direct supervisor again, am I right?"

"Yes."

"You have heard Dr. James' testimony that she went home and threw up as a reaction to being forced to have sex with you, is that correct?"

"Yes."

"But it's your sworn testimony that she was already ill when she left the Hyatt, am I right?"

"Yes."

"So, you're claiming that even though she was ill, she made it all the way home before she had to throw up, is that correct?"

"Yes, that must have been the case."

"Dr. James was pregnant when you had sex with you, was she not?"

"Yes, as a matter of fact, she told me she was."

"And your response was, 'I don't give a shit. Do you know how long I've wanted to fuck you,' wasn't it?"

"No, I never would have said that to her."

"So, you saw Dr. James naked. Did she look pregnant?"

"She was at that stage where you wouldn't want to ask because she might not be. She had lost her waist, but she was still beautiful, as I'm sure she still is."

"So, you had no hesitation having sex with her?"

"No, and she obviously had no hesitation having sex with me."

"Dr. Browning, you've heard Dr. James' testimony about your meeting the next morning, have you not?"

"Yes."

"And she has testified that the reason she was so angry was that you had promised her not to terminate Dr. Ryan's residency if she had sex with you, am I correct?"

"Yes, that was her testimony."

"But your claim is that you had discussed terminating his residency with her before that, and that you had made no promises to her that had anything to do with her having sex with you, is that right?"

"Yes, that's right."

"And that she was that angry the next morning about the termination of his residency without your having broken any promise to her relating to her having sex with you to prevent the termination?"

"Yes."

"In the seven years you have worked with Dr. James, have you ever seen her that angry?"

"No, not that I can recall."

"Are you married, Dr. Browning?"

"Yes."

"No further questions, your Honor."

It was 5:30. Having had two children of her own, Judge Weldon was mindful of Rene's condition, and actually had been surprised at how well she seemed to be holding up. Marilyn was very pleased that they had drawn a woman judge. No explaining necessary.

"Court will reconvene at 9:00 tomorrow morning. We are adjourned."

CHAPTER THIRTY-ONE

It was 7:00 in the evening and Rene was standing at the front desk of the local police precinct. She had called Marilyn, who said she would be there right away. Teddy had beaten Browning up in the courthouse parking lot. He had cold-cocked him as he walked to his car. Browning had called the police. Rene had already posted Teddy's bond. The door to the jail opened and Teddy walked out. Rene stepped up to him and put her arms tight around him.

"Oh, baby, what were you thinking?"

"Pretty obvious, isn't it?"

"Let me see your hands."

Teddy's knuckles were bruised and his hands were swollen.

"You're a surgeon. You just can't do this kind of thing."

"I don't give a shit. He hurt you and then lied about it."

"This is why I didn't tell you. This doesn't solve anything."

"It does for me."

Marilyn walked in. She gave both Rene and Teddy a hug.

"This isn't the first time I've had this happen," she said. "It's a normal reaction for men who want to protect the women in their lives. And it crosses all economic and social lines."

She turned to Rene. "It looks like you've bonded him out. Good."

"So, what do we do now?" asked Rene, who had never been in a police precinct before.

"I'm going to call Warren. I can't imagine that they'll want to follow through with this."

"Hello, Warren, this is Marilyn."

"Yes, I know your voice. So, what's going on?"

Marilyn told him she was at the precinct and filled him in.

"Not totally unexpected, as you know," Warren replied.

"So, I'm assuming you'll advise Browning not to follow through with this."

"I'll obviously have to talk with him. He hasn't called me. Probably embarrassed that he got the short end of it. Why didn't you talk with Teddy before this?"

"That clearly was my mistake. He just didn't seem like the type."

"There is no type, as you and I both know. I would have been tempted to beat the shit out of him, too. That's just between us, right?"

"Of course. Let me know as soon as you can on what you decide. I need to advise Teddy and Rene on where this is going."

Rene told Marilyn she was driving Teddy home. She iced his hands right away and leaned down and kissed them.

Marilyn called to say that Warren had convinced Browning not to press charges. Good news.

"Promise me you'll never do anything like that ever again."

"I can't."

"Why not?"

"Because I care about you way too much."

CHAPTER THIRTY-TWO

Court was back in session. Marilyn glanced over at Browning. He had a bruise on his cheek and a scrape on his chin, both on the side away from the jury. No black eye. Lucky guy.

"Defendants call Diane Livingston."

Diane Livingston took the stand and was sworn in.

"Ms. Livingston, are you employed by Kenton University?"

"Yes. I am the Assistant Human Resources Director for the medical school."

"How long have you held that position?"

"Four years."

"Did Dr. Rene James come to see you recently?"

"Yes, she did. She said it was important for her to see me right away. That was about two months ago."

"Did you know who she was?"

"Yes, she is well known in the medical school and in general at Kenton. That's why I made room in my schedule for her."

"So, you saw her in your office the day she contacted you, is that correct?"

"Yes, I met with her that afternoon."

"What did she discuss with you at that meeting?"

"She made a complaint of sexual harassment against Dr. Mark Browning, who is the Interim Chief of Surgery at the medical school."

"What was her complaint?"

"She said that Dr. Browning had forced her to have sex with him by threatening to terminate the residency of her baby's father if she didn't. She said she had had sex with Dr. Browning in response to the threat, but that he terminated Dr. Ryan anyway."

"So did you investigate Dr. James' complaint?"

"Yes."

"What did your investigation consist of?"

"I spoke with Dr. Browning, and detailed Dr. James' allegations against him. He admitted having sex with her, but claimed it was voluntary and that it had nothing to do with his decision to terminate Dr. Ryan's residency. I also spoke with Dr. Browning's assistant concerning what she observed about Dr. James' demeanor when she came to Dr. Browning's office the morning the residents' assignment list came out. In addition, I contacted the Hyatt to confirm that Dr. Browning had had a room reservation at the hotel on the night in question."

"Did you take any action with regard to Dr. James' allegations?"

"No."

"Why not?"

"I had known Dr. Browning for a long time, and I believed his denial. In addition, Dr. James didn't claim that she had been harmed financially or professionally by the conduct she complained about."

"So, you believe Dr. James had to make such a claim in order to state a valid sex harassment complaint, is that correct?"

"Yes, that's correct."

"No further questions, your Honor."

Marilyn stood for her cross.

"So, Ms. Livingston, it's your position and the university's position that Dr. James' sex harassment complaint only alleges illegal conduct if she was harmed financially or professionally, am I correct?"

"Yes, that's right."

"No further questions, your Honor."

CHAPTER THIRTY-THREE

"The defendants call Eric Andersen as a rebuttal witness".

Andersen walked to the front of the courtroom and took a seat in the witness stand. He was tall and dark with piercing blue eyes.

Marilyn turned to Rene and whispered, "Who the heck is Eric Andersen?" Rebuttal witnesses didn't have to be disclosed in advance.

"I was married to him a long time ago."

"Geez, Rene, you told me you've never been married."

"The marriage was annulled. I was told I could treat it as if it had never happened."

"Wrong advice. When were you married to this guy?"

"A dozen years ago."

How long were you married before it was annulled?"

"Six months."

"That's a long time in the annulment world. What were the grounds?"

"I didn't want to have children."

Kramer asked, "Mr. Andersen, please state your full name for the record."

"Eric Martin Andersen."

"What do you do for a living, Mr. Andersen?"

"I'm a producer for CBS News."

"How did you meet Dr. James?"

"I was assigned to produce a segment on her and her work restoring injured children's faces."

"So, she was already well known for her work when you met her?"

"Yes."

"Did you and Dr. James have a relationship at some point?"

"Yes, I was married to her."

"When were you divorced?"

"We were never divorced. The marriage was annulled."

"When was that?"

"Twelve years ago."

"What were the grounds for the annulment?"

"She refused to have children."

"Did you know that before you married her?"

"Yes, but I thought I could change her mind. I was unsuccessful."

"Dr. James has testified that men were intimidated by her. Did you observe that?"

"No, to the contrary. She had a number of men who were interested in her. I guess I was the one she fell for."

"Did you know when you married her that she didn't want to have children?"

"That's what she told me. But I thought she was in love with me and that I could change her mind. That obviously wasn't the case."

"No further questions, your Honor."

Marilyn stood. "Dr. James, would you please stand up."

Rene grabbed both arms of the chair and stood up.

"Mr. Andersen, from your observation, is Dr. James pregnant?"

"Yes."

"Does it make you a little angry that Dr. James is pregnant?"

"More than a little."

Bingo. Marilyn really was great.

Kramer stood up. "Your Honor. One more follow-up question. Mr. Andersen, do your feelings regarding Dr. James' pregnancy have any impact on the truthfulness of your testimony?"

"No."

The judge called a 20-minute recess. They walked out into the hall.

Andersen said, "Rene." She turned and walked over to him.

"I was subpoenaed."

"Yes, I know."

"How are you?"

"I'm feeling fine."

"I wish you and the baby all the best."

He leaned down to kiss her, and she turned her cheek. She walked back over to Marilyn.

"Do you still love him?"

"Not enough to be married to him."

CHAPTER THIRTY-FOUR

"Plaintiff calls Alice Ross."

Alice took the stand and was sworn in.

"Ms. Ross, were you married to Dr. Barry Ross, the former Chief of Surgery at Kenton Medical School?"

"Yes, Barry died of a heart attack about two months ago."

"And his interim replacement is Dr. Mark Browning, is he not?"

"Yes, that's correct."

"Do you know Dr. Rene James?"

"Yes, she is an Associate Professor in the Plastic and Reconstructive Surgery Department."

"Did you and your husband see Dr. James socially?"

"Yes, we would have dinner with her several times a year. She is a wonderful doctor and a wonderful person."

Whoa, thought Marilyn, that's an unexpected testimonial.

"Why do you say that?"

"The work she does with children and veterans is nationally known."

"Did Dr. James ever tell you that she had trouble meeting men?"

"Yes, although I found that hard to believe. She said men were intimidated by her. I guess I can understand it. She is not only good looking, she is very accomplished."

"At some point, did Dr. Ross have a conversation with you about Dr. James' relationships with residents?"

"Yes. He said Dr. James would greet the new residents at the beginning of the semester, which he encouraged because she was so well-known. She would invite a few of them to her home for dinner, and sometimes the relationships became more intimate. He didn't see a problem with it, since it was entirely voluntary and none of the residents ever complained. He emphasized that she never gave invitations to anyone she supervised."

"Do you know if Dr. Ross ever told Dr. James that this was a problem because she was an associate professor and they were residents?"

"He said he didn't."

"No further questions, your Honor."

Kramer stood and introduced himself.

"Ms. Ross, are you aware that Dr. James had sex with many of these residents?"

"Yes, I assumed so, although I never discussed it with her."

"And you saw no problem with that even though she was well above them in the medical school hierarchy?"

"Dr. James was not the kind of person who would do anything that would be harmful to any of them."

Now he's sorry he asked that one, Marilyn thought.

"No further questions, your Honor."

CHAPTER THIRTY-FIVE

The Judge called a 20-minute recess. Rene walked out into the hall. Teddy was waiting for her with a paper in his hand.

"Hi, how are you doing out here?" The witnesses were sequestered, which meant that they were excluded from the courtroom until the parties said that they would not be recalled.

"Better now that you're here. I want you to marry me right now. I have the license, and Judge Engel has agreed to perform the ceremony in his chambers."

"You're kidding."

"No. Right now."

"I'll obviously have to consult Marilyn."

Rene found Marilyn in the hall and told her what Teddy wanted to do. This case isn't boring, Marilyn thought.

Marilyn pondered the idea for a minute and couldn't come up with a downside. It would make Rene an 'honest woman' with jurors who still had problems with all the residents and do away with sting of the defendants' argument that she was just promiscuous and wanted sex whenever she wanted it.

"If this is what you want, you have my blessing," Marilyn said, and kissed Rene on the cheek.

"I'm not sure."

"Do you love him?"

"Yes. It's not just the sex. He's a really good guy."

"Then I guess the question is what you want for the baby."

"He's said from the beginning that he wanted the baby, and, surprisingly, his parents say they do, too. I'm just not sure I want to be married to anyone."

"What do you want on the baby's birth certificate? Does it matter to you?"

"You know, I think it actually does."

"Well then, I guess the choice is obvious. There's no annulment under these circumstances, but there's always divorce, and you know I'm here," Marilyn said with a smile.

Rene hugged Marilyn and walked back to Teddy.

"I'm ready."

"Judge Engel is waiting for us. Let's go."

They walked back to the judge's chambers and told his clerk they were there for the ceremony. The judge came out of his office with a wide smile on his face.

"This is one of the nicest things I'm required to do." He had performed the ceremony so often that he knew it by heart.

"I leave the 'obey' out unless the couple requests it."

"That's fine," said Teddy, before Rene could speak.

"Do you mind if the bailiff is the witness?"

"No, we'd appreciate it."

"Do you have a ring?"

"Yes," said Teddy, which was a surprise to Rene.

"It was my grandmother's." It was a platinum band with diamonds and sapphires. He had taken it to a jeweler with one of her rings to make sure it would fit.

"It's beautiful," she said.

The judge performed the familiar ceremony.

"You may kiss the bride." Teddy gave Rene a warm, soft kiss. She kissed him back. They walked back to Judge Weldon's courtroom as she took the bench.

Marilyn approached the bench. She indicated that she wanted Kramer to join her.

"Your Honor, Judge Engel has just married Dr. James and Dr. Ryan in his chambers. What would the defendants like us to do with that information?"

"Your Honor, I don't see how we cannot inform the jury."

"Ladies and gentlemen, the court and the parties would like to let you know that Judge Engel, who occupies the chambers next to mine, has just married Dr. James and Dr. Ryan in his chambers."

The jurors smiled.

CHAPTER THIRTY-SIX

Marilyn got them the honeymoon suite at the Ritz. She thought the Hyatt had too many other connotations at this point. She ordered Rene lingerie from Nordstrom for delivery in the early evening. She had known the Nordstrom sales associate for a long time, and she had always come through in a pinch. She also sent them a nice bottle of non-alcoholic Champagne, although she wasn't sure there was such a thing.

Teddy sensed that Rene was still not completely sure that her snap decision to marry him had been the correct one. She came out of the bathroom in her new lingerie. He didn't know how she could manage to look more beautiful, but she had. He popped the cork on the Champagne, poured two glasses and gave one to her.

"To us."

She hesitated, then looked straight at him and said, "To us."

Their sex had always been powerful, even while Rene was pregnant, but this night he was very tender with her, and he could tell from her kisses that his choice was appreciated.

They held each other in the large bed until the bell to the suite rang. Marilyn had sent them breakfast. She knew Rene would be hungry and wanted her alert and attentive from the beginning of the long day. Rene and Teddy both appreciated Marilyn's thoughtfulness. They knew that once they stepped out the door, it was off to the races again.

"Ladies and gentlemen, the parties have concluded their cases and submitted them to the court and to you." Judge Weldon summarized the law for the jury that they would be required to apply to the facts. "The attorneys for the parties will now present you with their closing arguments. Ms. Harris."

Marilyn stood and walked towards the jury. As a woman, she was able to stand closer to them than a larger man without intimidating them. All good jury trial lawyers knew that jurors felt confined to their chairs and couldn't move back if they felt uncomfortable. This was an advantage for a smaller woman, who could walk right up to the rail. Marilyn used no notes and looked directly at each juror.

"Ladies and gentlemen, this is the first time I've been able to talk to you directly since we began presenting the evidence in this case. Rene and I want to thank each of you personally for taking the time out of your busy lives to serve on this jury. This is the only major country in the world that still tries cases to juries. That's because we've learned over the years that, even though juries are time consuming, they bring a common sense to cases that judges and lawyers can't. And that's what we're asking you to do today. To look at the facts of this case and make a determination based on your own common sense as to who's telling the truth about what happened."

"The defendants will ask you to believe that Rene just wanted sex with lots of attractive men, and that when Dr. Browning was no longer her immediate supervisor, he became one of them. But, ladies and gentlemen, that narrative doesn't pass the common sense test.

"Rene's testimony shows that she was not just interested in sex, but in intimacy, which is something different. She told you that when she turned 50, which is a watershed age for women, she decided that she was not going to spend the rest of her life without 'male companionship.' Not without sex, but without male companionship, which is an important distinction. She had no husband and no children, and her family lived out of state. She had a 12-hour workday and a big investment house that she rattled around in."

"One thing Rene is not is a stupid woman. She had a spectacular career, but no personal life. She could have slept with many of the married men she worked with, but that was an unacceptable solution for her because it wasn't just sex she wanted. She found herself in the same situation as many successful women— eligible men were uninterested in a relationship with her. She wasn't sure exactly why. She was good looking and successful, but it was a fact. Rene's former husband has testified that she had no trouble meeting eligible men, but they had been married a dozen years ago before she was nationally famous for her work and well before she was 50."

Marilyn continued. "Rene had noticed, however, that for whatever reason, younger men were not intimidated by her. Perhaps because they had their entire careers ahead of them, and they imagined themselves becoming as successful as she was. She had had residents show an interest in her many times, but had never taken them up on it. But then at 50, something said, 'why not?'"

"She also felt, however, that she didn't want to tie any of them to a woman who was old enough to be their mother, which she had no illusions about. And so when she met the new residents that year at the beginning of the semester, she gave a few of them she was interested in getting to know better a slip of paper with her name and phone number on it, along with the word 'Dinner.'

"She had no idea what the response would be, but as she stated in her testimony, they all called her. Had they been older, she thought, she wouldn't have heard from any of them. She met them all for dinner and then they went to bed. This intimacy, she felt, was better than none. She was fond of all of them, but she and they knew permanent relationships were not in the picture because of her age.

"We are asking you to set aside the usual stereotypes we apply to women in our culture. As Rene asked Mr. Kramer, would you ask these questions of her if she were a man? If she were a man, we would be congratulating her on her prowess rather than judging her for 'sleeping around.' And we would not assume that because she slept with some men, she wanted to sleep with others, including Browning.

"Rene learned later from the Chief of Surgery that he knew about this arrangement, but never saw a problem with it because she never directly supervised any of them and none of them ever complained. He saw it more as something they enjoyed in their high-pressure lives, and as Dr. Mastrangelo testified, she was, in fact, a beautiful woman."

"The arrangement went well for everyone for five semesters until it didn't. Rene was going through menopause and her birth control didn't work as it was supposed to. Her primary physician confirmed that she was pregnant, which was a major shock to her. She had to decide whether to tell the father and, more importantly, whether to terminate the pregnancy. And why wouldn't she? She was 52, single, and had a job that was very demanding physically. And she could go back to her everyday life as if nothing had happened. But this is where intimacy comes in again. Contrary to everyone's advice, she decided to keep the baby. And why? Because this would be someone who would be with her when she was 60, 70, 80, and beyond.

"And then, the other shoe dropped. Barry Ross, the Chief of Surgery, had a heart attack and died, and Rene's immediate supervisor, Mark Browning, became the interim chief. Not only had Dr. Browning always been jealous of Rene's renown, he had also always wanted to sleep with her. Dr. Ross had had no problem with Rene's resident arrangement, and in fact, had known about it and tacitly encouraged it. But Dr. Browning called Rene into his office and told her that Dr. Ryan would have to find another residency, since she technically supervised him. Unless they could find another solution. When she asked what that would be, he handed her a hotel room key.

"Here's where intimacy comes in again. She was not only carrying Dr. Ryan's baby, he had told her he was in love with her, and she didn't want him to leave her. And so, at five months pregnant, she was willing to humiliate and degrade herself by having sex with Dr. Browning, even oral sex, in order to protect Dr. Ryan's residency, even though she knew Browning's proposition was illegal."

"But she learned the next morning that Dr. Browning had gone back on his word and that he had terminated Dr. Ryan's residency. Dr. Browning has testified that he was going to terminate Dr. Ryan's residency anyway, but that's where your common sense comes in. Why did Rene agree to have sex with Browning the night before the residents' assignments came out? And why did she throw up once she got home, as Dr. Ryan has testified, even though she was just fine the next morning? And why was she so very angry with Dr. Browning the next morning as Denise Perkins, Dr. Browning' assistant, has testified? And, by the way, Ms. Perkins has no reason to lie. In fact, it is against her best interest not to support her boss."

"Rene reported Browning to the university's Human Resources Vice President, Diane Livingston, that afternoon. Ms. Livingston testified that she investigated Rene's claims by talking with Dr. Browning and his assistant, Denise Perkins, but did not believe Rene's claims. She mistakenly believed that Rene had to allege financial or professional damage to state a valid sex harassment claim. But, ladies and gentlemen, that is not the law, as Judge Weldon has instructed you. As a result, the university has violated the law by not taking any action against Dr. Browning, and is liable to Rene for the maximum damages available to her under both Title VII and state law.

"As to Dr. Browning, Rene is asking that the damages awarded against him be large enough to deter him and any one like him from ever humiliating and degrading another employee in the way he has humiliated and degraded her. She is asking for a million dollars."

"Thank you, ladies and gentlemen, for your time and attention. Both Rene and I hope you will right this wrong."

CHAPTER THIRTY-SEVEN

Warren stood up and approached the jury box. As an experienced trial lawyer, he knew just where to stand. Like Marilyn, he had no notes. He knew this was his chance to talk directly to the jurors and he wasn't going to waste it.

"Ladies and gentlemen, because the plaintiff has to prove her case, she is given the chance to talk to you first. Marilyn Harris is an excellent attorney, and she has presented the plaintiff's case forcefully. But the university and Dr. Browning are asking you to take a second look at what's going on here. Dr. James would have you believe that, despite her good looks and success, she is unable to find appropriate men, and so she had to devise a way to find attractive, available men to have sex with. She says that's because she wasn't going to spend the rest of her life without 'male companionship.' To this the defendants say, 'Get a dog.'"

Marilyn knew he had just given her the perfect comeback for her rebuttal argument, which she was permitted because Rene had the burden of proof.

"This case only came about because Dr. James slipped up. For whatever reason, her birth control stopped working and she got pregnant. Around the same time, the Chief of Surgery, Barry Ross, who knew about her arrangement with the residents but looked the other way, died, and Dr. Browning, her immediate supervisor, was made the interim chief. Dr. Browning testified that he had always been attracted to Dr. James, but that he respected her position of never having sexual relations with her immediate supervisor. But then, all of a sudden, Dr. Browning wasn't her immediate supervisor anymore."

"Dr. Browning has testified that following Dr. Ross's death and his promotion to Chief of Surgery, Dr. James' demeanor changed. She made it clear to him that she was open to a sexual encounter. A night at the Hyatt to congratulate him on his promotion."

"Why did Dr. James' demeanor change? We really don't know. Had she been attracted to Dr. Browning all along, and now finally felt free to act on her feelings? Or did she see this as a career opportunity to ingratiate herself with her new Chief of Surgery, whom she knew wanted to sleep with her? We don't know, and neither did Dr. Browning. But he really didn't care. He just knew that, for whatever reason, she was finally making herself available to him, and he wasn't going to pass up the opportunity."

"And so, Dr. Browning and Dr. James met at the Hyatt Hotel as they have both testified. But that's where their stories diverge. Dr. James claims that she only showed up because she was trying to protect Dr. Ryan's residency, as Dr. Browning had promised, and that she was willing to have sex with Dr. Browning to do that. But her testimony also shows that sex was not a big deal for her. In fact, she had had sex with a number of residents over the last couple of years at her invitation. The defendants believe it's clear that Dr. James had sex with Dr. Browning because she wanted to and not because she was forced to, as she claims."

"Studies show, surprisingly, that men are actually more romantic than women. Dr. Browning didn't just want to have sex with Dr. James. He wanted to make love to her, and had wanted to for a long time. She says she was surprised that he helped her get dressed when she was leaving, but his feelings for her were no surprise to him. The juxtaposition of their encounter and the issuance of the resident assignment list had never occurred to him. He just wanted to be with her as soon as he could."

"Dr. James says she was so angry with Dr. Browning the next morning because he had gone back on his promise not to terminate Dr. Ryan's residency if she had sex with him. But Dr. Browning testified he had already told Dr. James that Dr. Ryan would have to leave, and that although she may have been certain their amazing sex would make it very difficult for him to follow through, something that he admitted to her, he had no choice if he wanted to keep his position."

"Dr. James contacted Ms. Harris about her claim of sexual harassment that same day, along with Ms. Livingston, the Assistant Human Resources Director for the Medical School, who agreed to see Dr. James right away. Ms. Livingston knew of Dr. James and that she was a highly respected surgeon in the

Medical School. Ms. Livingston testified that Dr. James related all her claims against Dr. Browning to her, but that when she spoke with Dr. Browning, she believed his denials. Dr. Browning hopes you do, too.

"So why would Dr. James pick then to have sex with Dr. Browning? The question quickly becomes, 'Why not?' Studies show that a woman's desire for sex increases during the second trimester of pregnancy. Why, we don't know, but it's a fact. In any case, Dr. James certainly wasn't averse to sex at that point. And she's already established through her testimony that sex was an important part of her life. So why not enjoy something that she very well may have wanted for a long time?"

Marilyn had instructed Rene not to react to the defendants' closing, but she could tell Rene was having a hard time with that. Marilyn put her hand on Rene's arm and smiled at her.

"And so, ladies and gentlemen, Dr. Browning is asking you to question why we are really here. Is it because Dr. Browning coerced Dr. James into having sex with him under false pretenses, or because Dr. James, as a result of her good looks and success, was used to getting her way and Dr. Browning didn't give it to her?"

"Dr. Browning and the university are asking you to find that they have not violated the law, and that they have not allowed Dr. James to be sexually harassed and discriminated against because of her sex."

CHAPTER THIRTY-EIGHT

Marilyn stood with a smile on her face. "Ladies and gentlemen, Dr. James and I both want you to know that she *does* have a dog—a black lab named Jake." The jury smiled.

"Mr. Kramer and Dr. Browning would have you believe that Dr. James went to the Hyatt Hotel voluntarily that night at 9:00 p.m. at five months pregnant to have a roll in the hay with Dr. Browning, either because she wanted him that much or because she wanted to further her career. This while she was already living with her baby's father, to whom she is now married."

"Rene and I have asked you from the beginning to use your common sense. Rene was already living with Dr. Ryan, who is now her husband, and who has testified that he is very much in love with her. And it should be clear to you and all of us that Dr. James needs no help from Dr. Browning or anyone else in furthering her stellar career. In fact, she knew Dr. Browning had a history of doing his best to undermine her, although he admits with no success."

"Or does it make more sense that, at five months pregnant, Rene wanted Dr. Ryan to be with her, and that she was willing to do whatever she believed she needed to do to keep him with her, even if it meant having sex, including oral sex, with a man she didn't want to have sex with."

"In our culture, we still believe that, unlike men, women who enjoy having intimate relations with more than one man have a moral flaw. This goes back to the day when the only way to identify a baby's father was to be sure the mother had only had sex with one man. Although that day is long gone, we still carry that baggage around with us today, and even brilliant, accomplished women like Rene are the victims of it. In fact, that's what the defendants want you to believe about her. If she were a man, we wouldn't even be discussing it. We would be congratulating her on her interesting personal life."

"And let's be clear. Just because a woman wants to have sex with one man doesn't mean she wants to have sex with another. In other words, just because Rene wanted to have intimate relations with other men didn't mean she automatically consented to sex with Dr. Browning. And Dr. Browning knew that, which is why he gave her the room key."

Marilyn held up the key.

"Judge Weldon has told you about something called 'quid pro quo,' which translated from the Latin, means 'this for that.' That's exactly what this case is about. If Rene gave Dr. Browning sex, the 'this,' he would allow Dr. Ryan to stay, the 'that.' Ladies and gentlemen, that's illegal under Title VII, the law that prohibits sex discrimination and sex harassment."

"Ask yourself why Rene would put herself through this under the circumstances if she were just making it all up. There's a movie called *Network* where the main character says, 'I'm mad as hell, and I'm not going to take it anymore.' That's what Rene is telling you with this lawsuit. We are asking you not to make her take it anymore."

Marilyn sat down and took Rene's hand.

142

CHAPTER THIRTY-NINE

Judge Weldon addressed the jury.

"Ladies and gentlemen, the parties have presented their cases to you. Now your real work begins. I am going to review with you the instructions the parties have agreed upon and I have approved for you. You are required to follow these instructions in reaching your verdict."

"I'm sure many of you have watched trials on television, most of which are in criminal cases. In criminal cases, the burden of proof is beyond a reasonable doubt. That is not the case here. This is a civil case where Plaintiff James is only required to prove that it is more likely than not that the facts she and others who testified in support of those facts are true. It is your job as jurors to make that determination based upon the testimony you have heard in this courtroom. It is your job to assess the credibility of each of the witnesses and to determine what weight, if any, to give to their testimony. You are required to apply the law as I have instructed you, whether you agree with it or not."

Judge Weldon proceeded to lay out the required elements of claims of sex harassment and sex discrimination against the university under the federal law, and of the state law claims of assault and battery and infliction of emotional distress against Dr. Mark Browning, being careful to remind the jury that assault and battery did not require a violent act, but merely unwelcome touching. She also outlined the requirements of the state law claim of negligent retention against the university, which involved Browning's harassing conduct.

"Your first task when you enter the jury room will be to select a foreperson. You may then begin your deliberations. You have been provided with verdict forms approved by me and agreed upon by the parties to guide you in your deliberations. If you have questions during your deliberations, please provide them to the bailiff and he will forward them to me. If you are an alternate juror, we appreciate your service and hope you have found it interesting and informative. You are now dismissed."

The jurors filed out of the jury box and into the jury room.

Judge Weldon then addressed the attorneys and the parties.

"Counsel and the parties must make themselves available at all times by cellphone and should not leave the courthouse. You will be notified as soon as the jury reaches a verdict and should return to the courtroom as quickly as possible upon receiving such notice. You may remain in the courtroom if you wish, but you are not required to."

Judge Weldon turned and entered her chambers, along with her staff.

Marilyn was sure at this point that her decision to proceed with the trial while Rene was pregnant was the correct one from a strategic perspective, but was having second thoughts about the personal toll the trial might be having on Rene. She had consulted with Rene on more than one occasion about the stress inherent in a trial, and Rene had always assured her that she could handle it. But Marilyn understood from past experience that there were few things more stressful than waiting for a jury to return. Lawyers who handled jury trials on a regular basis almost always drank too much because there was almost no way of accurately predicting what a jury would find.

Marilyn had told Rene to bring some reading materials. Predictably, she had brought a medical journal and a baby book. She asked if she could call her office. Marilyn said of course. She had already told Rene there was no predicting how long the jury would be out, which Rene communicated to her staff. Rene was still the best facial reconstruction surgeon anywhere, and there were patients waiting for her. Teddy came around the rail and sat next to her. His concern was almost palpable, which confirmed to Marilyn that she had been right about him. Marilyn told both of them that it would probably be a long afternoon.

Teddy called Gerry and gave him an update. Gerry asked specific questions about how Rene was holding up, and instructed him to get back to him right away if anything changed. Gerry was more concerned about the stress than he had let on to Rene or Marilyn. Rene had assured him that she felt physically able to proceed with the trial, and that Marilyn knew from her years of experience what she was doing. He knew how strong Rene was both mentally and physically, but only hoped it was enough.

Just two hours had passed when the bailiff indicated that the jury had reached a verdict. Judge Weldon emerged from her chambers and took the bench. The jury filed in. Rene motioned to Teddy.

"Call Gerry and tell him 15."

"Fifteen what?"

"Between contractions. Ask him whether he thinks it's false labor or the real thing."

Teddy hurried out of the courtroom and called Gerry. Gerry said he'd be there right away.

Marilyn and Rene stood and Marilyn put her arm around her. Teddy came back into the courtroom.

The foreperson, a woman, handed the verdict to the bailiff, who passed it to Judge Weldon. She read it and handed it back to the bailiff. Marilyn thought she detected an almost imperceptible smile. The bailiff returned the verdict to the Foreperson.

"Madam Foreperson, please publish the verdict."

"We, the jury, find in favor of Plaintiff Rene James and against Defendant Kenton University in the amount of two million dollars."

Marilyn felt Rene's knees buckle and sat down with her.

"We, the jury, find in favor of Plaintiff Rene James and against Defendant Mark Browning in the amount of one million dollars."

Judge Weldon addressed the jury. "Ladies and gentlemen, the parties and the court thank you for your unwavering attention and your carefully considered verdict. You can be proud of your contribution to our judicial system. You may speak to counsel for the parties, but are under no obligation to do so. You are dismissed."

The jury filed out.

"Mr. Kramer, do you have a motion?"

"Yes, your Honor, the defendants move for Judgment Notwithstanding the Verdict."

"Please submit your brief and the court will consider your motion."

"What's that all about?" asked Rene.

"The defendants are asking the court to set aside the jury's verdict. It won't happen, so don't worry, but Warren had to make the motion."

CHAPTER FORTY

Kramer came over and congratulated Marilyn. "Great job, as usual. You know we'll appeal." She did, although it was very difficult to overturn a jury verdict unless the court had made obvious errors, and Marilyn hadn't seen any.

Marilyn and Rene gave each other a long hug.

"We did it. Can you believe it?" asked Marilyn.

"I always believed it and you," Rene whispered. "I'm having contractions. Teddy has called Gerry and he's on his way. I'm not sure whether it's false labor or the real thing."

"Geez, Rene, when did they start? How frequent?"

"About a half an hour ago. Every 15 minutes."

"You didn't say anything!"

"I knew it was a bad time, and I'm still not sure it's real labor. Gerry should be here any minute."

Marilyn knew the media would be swarming outside, and hoped Gerry could make it through.

Gerry walked into the back of the courtroom and came immediately over to Rene. Teddy walked with him.

"Shit, Rene, you know this is what I've been afraid of."

"We won, Gerry, we won! Isn't that what we both wanted? It may well have gone the other way if I weren't pregnant. At least that's what Marilyn and I both think."

Marilyn hadn't expected Rene to include herself. She took a deep breath.

"How often are the contractions now?"

"Every 10 minutes. How do we know it's real labor?"

"Because the contractions are regular and getting closer together."

"Is there any way to stop them?"

"An alcohol drip sometimes works."

"How about a martini?"

"Rene, I really do love you," he said, trying not to laugh. "We need to go right now. My car is out front." He had put his medical shield in the front window.

"I'll go first," Marilyn said. Teddy and Gerry followed her on either side of Rene.

Marilyn stepped out into the media crowd. "Ladies and gentlemen, Dr. James is obviously very pleased with the verdict, and she would have been out to speak with you all sooner, but she is having labor contractions. Her doctor's car is out front, and we would greatly appreciate an unobstructed pathway. We will keep you posted on developments in the baby watch. Thanks so much for your consideration."

The Red Sea parted, although the cameras kept rolling as Gerry and Teddy helped Rene down the steps to the car. The cameras loved her regardless. Gerry had years of experience getting to the hospital quickly and he used all of it. He called ahead to confirm a room and explain the situation.

CHAPTER FORTY-ONE

They knew Rene at the hospital, where she performed her surgery and where she had a reputation for showing consideration for the staff. They got her a room right away. Gerry wanted her to have reached at least eight months before she had the baby. She was right there.

Gerry had asked his friend and colleague, Dan Cohen, who was a highly-respected ob-gyn, to assist him with Rene's delivery, and she had welcomed that. She had told Gerry she wanted to avoid a C-section, if at all possible, even though they always scheduled patients her age for one. He had agreed, but wanted Dan available for one just in case.

Teddy came in and Gerry had filled him in on Rene's status and the fact that he thought the baby was coming. Gerry went up to Rene's room.

"How often?"

"Every 2 minutes."

Gerry checked her out. She was almost completely dilated. He called for a gurney right away.

"You're almost fully dilated. The baby is clearly coming. I've called for a gurney stat. It's probably too late for an epidural to take effect in time. The anesthesiologist I've requested does a really good spinal with no side effects. Don't be unnecessarily brave."

"I'm going to tough it out. I think that's better for the baby."

"Are you a 100% sure?"

"100%."

The gurney arrived and they lifted her onto it. Gerry walked beside it to the elevator, which took them down to the delivery room where Teddy and Dan were waiting.

Teddy took her hand and kissed her.

She looked at him and smiled. "It's showtime. Your daughter is on the way."

They moved her to the delivery table. There was no indication that a C-section would be necessary and Rene had instructed them not to do an episiotomy, so Dan stood with Gerry beside the table. Rene was still glad he was there.

Rene's abdominal muscles were strong, and the baby wasn't large, so it only took a few good pushes and there Amanda was. Amanda had been Teddy's grandmother's name, and it was her ring that he had given to Rene. She had Rene's auburn hair and everyone assumed her blue eyes. But when she finally opened her eyes, they were Teddy's unusual green. A beautiful combination. Gerry put her on Rene's chest, and Teddy cut the cord with the skill of a surgeon. Rene saw that Teddy was crying. The nurses took Amanda to weigh and measure her, and Teddy kissed Rene again.

"Her temperature is down a little," said Gerry. "We can put her in an incubator, or you can take off your gown and shirt and hold her."

"I'll hold her," Teddy said. He put Amanda on his chest and wrapped his arms around her. Rene looked at him and knew for sure that for once, she'd made the right choice.

CHAPTER FORTY-TWO

Rene wanted to go home as soon as possible, but Gerry insisted that she spend the night to make sure the breast feeding was going well, and the hospital had agreed. Teddy slept on the pull-out sofa in the room, and the nurse brought Amanda into the room in her bassinet. Both Rene and Amanda slept well.

Teddy opened his eyes in the morning to the sight of Rene sitting up in bed nursing the baby. He had not expected the intensity of the reaction he had to seeing them together.

"Hello, love. Are you okay?"

"More than okay. How are my girls?"

He stepped over to Rene, kissed her and sat down on the edge of the bed.

Rene took his hand and put it on Amanda's head. "You have a beautiful daughter."

"And a beautiful wife."

"She's eating really well, so they're kicking us out. Faye is on the way to help us get out of Dodge."

There was a knock on the door just as she spoke. It was Faye with a wheelchair.

"Hi, Mom and Dad. I know, Rene, but they won't discharge you unless you use it. Let's get you dressed. They're waiting for you at the house." She walked over to Amanda and kissed her. "And Amanda is beautiful, as everyone expected."

Rene had never imagined that the four-bedroom house would ever be full, but now it was. Faye was in one bedroom and Amanda in another, and Rene's mother, who was still in shock over the marriage and the baby, was in the fourth. Even the garage was full with Teddy and Faye's cars. Plus, Teddy liked swimming in the pool where Jake joined him. Rene was almost as shocked as her mother by how it had all happened.

Faye announced that she was making her renowned pot roast for dinner. "There's nobody that doesn't like a good pot roast. With a nice red wine. It was one of the president's favorites."

"I'm guessing he's missing you."

"I'm guessing he is, too."

Rene didn't know what had happened, but she knew he'd made a mistake, and that she had benefited from it.

CHAPTER FORTY-THREE

Rene hadn't checked her phone all morning. It was filled with congratulatory voicemails, texts, and emails on both the case and the baby. Sandwiched in the middle was a transcribed voicemail message from the office of the president of the university congratulating her and asking her to call his office. It occurred to her that she ought to respond to that one first.

William Foster had been president for less than a year. He had replaced Faye's old boss, whom Rene knew well. Rene had met him a few times and had been initially impressed, but had no long-term personal insights. She was sure he was calling her because of the lawsuit.

"Rene, it's so nice to talk with you again. Congratulations on your new baby and on your legal victory, although I don't know whether I should really be saying that."

"You can count on the fact that that's just between us. I appreciate your taking the time to call. I'm familiar with your schedule."

"Listen, Rene, I know you're very busy right now, too, so I'll get right to the point. We would like to offer you the position of Chief of Surgery in the Medical School. I know you will need to consider the offer carefully and discuss it with your family and colleagues, but I would like to hear back from you as soon as possible."

Rene paused. She was stunned.

"Thank you, Dr. Foster."

"Oh, please call me Bill."

"Thank you, Bill. I'll get back to you as soon as I can."

Rene called Marilyn as soon as she ended the call.

"Marilyn, they've offered me the Chief of Surgery position."

Marilyn laughed. "Brilliant move."

"Why do you say that?"

"Think about it. They know you're highly unlikely to accept the position with a new baby and your surgical practice. So then they can counter the bad publicity they're getting because of their loss in the case by claiming they've offered you this prestigious position, but that you've turned it down."

"Wow. You're right. So, what now?"

"We need to think strategy. This is clearly Warren's idea. There's got to be a way to use this to our advantage."

Marilyn called Warren. He answered.

"Hi, Marilyn, I've missed you."

"Hi, Warren, you've always been a charming SOB."

"Didn't work this time. How can I help you?"

"I'm calling about the offer."

"What offer?"

"Come on, Warren, don't play dumb with me. We've known each other too long."

"Okay, you got me. So when will she respond?"

"We've obviously got to have time to discuss her options."

"Soon?"

"Yes, soon."

CHAPTER FORTY-FOUR

Marilyn called Rene the next morning to tell her she'd talked with Warren and that he had admitted coming up with the idea for the offer.

"How is the little one?"

"She's terrific. Teddy has her right now. He's besotted. And the grandparents are everywhere. Faye is even trying to teach my mother how to cook."

"Any thoughts on how to proceed?"

"You were right that it's an almost impossible situation. It's an amazing offer, but I can't figure out how I can take it."

"That's exactly what they're counting on. Why don't you give Alice a call? She'll know all the dirty details."

She called Alice. "Hi, Alice, I have something to ask you about."

"Hi, sweetheart, I was waiting until this afternoon to call to give you a little breathing room. I've seen the pictures of Amanda. She's beautiful."

"Yes, we're over the moon. Who would have predicted any of this? Listen, I have something I want to talk to you about."

"You know I'll help in any way I can."

"They've offered me the chief's position. Marilyn thinks it's because they know I can't take it. I'm calling you to find out all the bad stuff."

"What a surprise!"

"Yes, it was to me, too, as you can imagine."

"I wouldn't put it past them to have offered it to you because they don't think you can take it. They know it's a tough spot and that you have a new baby."

"So tell me what's tough about it. Be honest."

"It's very political. You know surgeons aren't people oriented and that they all have big egos. You're the exception, which is why I've always really liked you. They all want more money for themselves and power for their programs. The chief has to deal with all that on a regular basis. And there is a lot of administrative work. It creates lots of stress. I think that's finally what got Barry."

"Would I still be able to do my surgery?"

"Maybe. He was able to continue much of his. But he didn't have a new baby."

"That's the issue isn't it, although you know I'm a strong person."

"Yes, I do, but that may not be enough. And you know that even though Teddy obviously loves the baby, his residency is very demanding. They know that."

"Well, Alice, keep thinking."

"I will, and by the way, I need to say that I think you'd be wonderful in the job, just for the reasons I've mentioned."

Rene called Marilyn and told her what Alice had said. Marilyn agreed.

"Listen," said Marilyn, "I have an idea. This verdict will not be overturned, so you're eventually going to get a lot of money out of the lawsuit even after taxes. What if you agreed to pay for the salary and benefits for a full-time assistant to handle all the administrative work associated with the chief's job?"

"What a great idea. Do you think they'll go for it?"

"Maybe, especially if we publicize the offer."

CHAPTER FORTY-FIVE

Rene needed to talk with Teddy. He had to be on board with it all or she wouldn't go forward. She'd told him about the offer, and he'd told her he'd support her whatever she decided, but she wasn't sure he knew exactly what that meant. She found him in the nursery with Amanda, which somehow made it more difficult for her to bring it all up.

"Hello, darling. Amanda's obviously in love with you."

"And me with her. She's amazing."

"As are you. Just so you know, I'm really crazy about you."

"It's mutual."

She walked over and kissed both of them.

"Marilyn and I have been talking. She's had an idea about how I can manage the chief's position. She thinks I should offer to pay the salary and benefits for a full-time assistant to handle the administrative duties the chief is responsible for. She's sure we'll get enough money from the lawsuit to do that. The question, of course, is whether they'll agree to that since they really want me to turn down the offer. And even if they do agree, whether that will allow me enough time for Amanda and my practice, both of which are obviously extremely important to me."

"I wish I had the answer," Teddy said, shaking his head. "What I want most is for you to be happy. We hadn't expected any of this, and neither one of us knows exactly how to juggle it. I just know that I love you, and we have to keep trying to find a way to handle it all."

She didn't know quite how she ended up with this guy, but she couldn't have wished for anyone better.

She called Marilyn. "Make them the offer. I think we can make this work, but we need to know if they'll bite."

"I agree. If they won't, then we'll have to find another route. Despite what I've often told you, I now think there are other universities that would hire you."

That was certainly news to Rene. She wasn't sure why Marilyn had changed her mind on that, but it was clearly something they needed to discuss.

Marilyn called Warren. "Hi, Warren, I think we may have a solution. I know your plan was for Rene to turn this offer down, but she's willing to pay the salary and benefits for a full-time assistant to help her with the administrative aspects of the chief's position if the university will agree. It would still be a big PR coup for the university if she stayed on, and I can assure you she'd do a bang-up job. She'd, of course, want to continue with her surgery, but she and I both think she could do that if she had this assistance. Keep in mind that having a woman Chief of Surgery would be a big recruiting advantage for the medical school."

"Wow, Marilyn, I think you've just one-upped me. We really should practice together. We'd be unbeatable."

"Maybe so, but I need a response to Rene's proposal first."

"I'll run it by them no later than tomorrow. I'll get back to you then."

Marilyn recapped the conversation for Rene, adding, "I want to prepare you for a no," she told her. "I know Kenton doesn't like to be challenged, and the fact we're both women isn't going to help with the Board."

Rene really was curious about Marilyn's comment about other universities possibly being interested in her after she'd sued Kenton, something Marilyn had always dismissed out of hand in the past.

"You know I respect your opinion on just about everything," Rene said. "So why have you changed your thinking on how this lawsuit would have alienated other universities?"

"That's certainly a fair question under the circumstances, and in the past, I would have advised my university clients not to touch you with an 11-foot pole. But I have gotten to know you extremely well over the past few months under a variety of circumstances, and I believe I have learned things about you that would allow me to advocate for you in ways I couldn't for others."

"Well, that's certainly flattering, especially coming from you."

"Yes it is, and it's meant to be. But I don't want you to think other universities will be beating down your door. Despite your obvious abilities, you will still be damaged goods in the opinions of many in power at universities around the country. So, let's not get ahead of ourselves. Let's see what we can do with what we've got. Warren has been the university's lawyer for a long time, and if I can convince him of the wisdom of our proposal, we will probably prevail here."

"I know you have known each other for a long time, and that you do respect each other," Rene said.

"Yes, and he knows I wouldn't urge him to do anything that would damage him with the university. That gives us a real edge here. And I really believe our proposal is a win for both sides, something that is very hard to find. I think he may see that, too. I've talked with him many times about what an asset you are to the university, and I believe he understands that now."

"Will you let me know as soon as you hear anything?"

"Of course I will."

CHAPTER FORTY-SIX

Marilyn's phone rang in the middle of the night. It was Warren.

"Hey, Warren, what's going on?"

"Not much. You alone?"

"Yes, you?"

"Yes. We need to talk about Rene. I've got two old guys on the Board who are going to trash her proposal. I told them she wouldn't take the chief's job because she wanted to keep cutting on people and she had a new baby. But now she says she's willing to pay for an assistant with what they say is the university's money."

"Warren, have you had a drink?"

"Yes, more than one. How about you?"

"Yes, but only one."

"So, you're brilliant. What do I do with them? I want this to work. I think it's a good way to deal with the bad publicity her fucking case has caused the school and that's hanging around my neck. Do you want me to come over?"

"Not right now. Listen, tell them it's her money now, and she's willing to pay some of it back for a productive employee that will cost them nothing."

"They both say they would have fucked her, too, and they don't know why she's entitled to any money for that."

"Explain that a jury decided what happened to her was a violation of the current law, and that the verdict is not going to be overturned, whether they agree with it or not, so they might as well have her pay some of the money back by spending it to hire an employee who will contribute to the university."

"You really are brilliant, Marilyn. I'm almost not mad that I lost to you. Are you sure you don't want me to come over?"

"I'm sure. Get some sleep. And try to remember what we've talked about."

"I'll call you tomorrow."

"Great. Rene is waiting for their decision."

Marilyn called Rene the next morning to let her know she'd spoken with Warren and that they might have hit a snag.

"Warren called me late last night to let me know that two of the Board members who had only agreed to make you the offer because he had guaranteed you'd turn it down are now balking at making it easier for you to take it. I won't tell you what he said they said, but they feel rewarding you for being disloyal to the university is not something they want to do. I gave him some good arguments to present to them, but they're not meeting until lunch, so we won't know until then."

"So where do we go from here if they reject the proposal?"

"You haven't been terminated, so you just go back to where you were, which wouldn't be awful, although it would most likely be uncomfortable in the department. And as we've discussed, I can start putting out some feelers for you. You really do have a lot to offer another program somewhere else. And there's no question that accepting the offer would still present some real difficulties, as we both know."

"So when will we know?

"As soon as I hear back from Warren, which should be in the early afternoon. I may just come over. I would like to see the baby."

"I'd like that. I miss seeing you."

CHAPTER FORTY-SEVEN

Marilyn pulled into the driveway of Rene's imposing house. Marilyn had a beautiful high-rise condo with a spectacular view, and had never understood Rene's desire for this place. But the house was clearly a beehive of activity when she arrived. Rene greeted Marilyn at the door holding Amanda.

"Oh, my God, Rene. Could she be any more beautiful? It was all worth it, wasn't it?"

"And she probably won the case for us. You always had confidence that she and I could do it."

"I wasn't so sure at the end, but you really did do it." They hugged and Marilyn kissed Amanda.

They walked into the family room where everyone was assembled. Rene gave Marilyn a glowing introduction. They were all familiar with her role in the legal victory, and were happy to put a face with the name.

"My breasts are telling me it's lunch time. I know you'll excuse me." Rene came back in a few minutes with Amanda nursing. She really was a good eater.

Faye came out of the kitchen to let them all know lunch was ready. Rene hadn't known what a really good cook Faye was when she hired her. It had certainly been a welcome surprise.

They were just finishing lunch when Marilyn's phone rang. She answered immediately.

"Hi, Warren. What's the news?"

"I just wanted to give you an update. No decision yet, but I have a feeling we might be getting there. Thanks for your suggestions last night."

"Glad you remembered them. I'm over at Rene's house. Let us know as soon as you can."

"That was Warren giving me an update" Marilyn said to the group. "They're still talking."

They all walked back into the family room. Teddy offered everyone a glass of sherry. Marilyn knew Rene well enough now to tell that she had tensed up. She walked over to her and put her arm around her shoulders. They both knew from Warren's call that it wasn't a done deal. They all drank their Sherry and talked about the baby.

Rene's phone rang unexpectedly. "This is Rene."

"This is Bill Foster. How are you, chief?"

"I beg your pardon?"

"The Board has agreed to your proposal. You're the new Chief of Surgery."

"You're not serious."

"I sure am. Congratulations!"

Marilyn had never seen Rene cry before, but she was crying now. Rene handed the phone to Marilyn.

"Hello, this is Marilyn Harris. Hi, Bill, I'm assuming you're the bearer of good tidings. That's terrific news! So what are the next steps? I'm sure you'll let us know. We'll talk soon. Yes, I'll tell her how pleased you are."

Rene handed Amanda to Teddy and gave Marilyn a big hug. Everyone cheered. Faye got the champagne that Teddy had bought out of the fridge and opened it. They all raised their glasses and toasted Rene and Marilyn and Amanda. It had been quite a day. It had been quite a year.